A DEAL FOR AMOS

A DEAL FOR AMOS

by

Vic J. Hanson

Dales Large Print Books
Long Preston, North Yorkshire,
England.

British Library Cataloguing in Publication Data.

Hanson, Vic J.
  A deal for Amos.

  A catalogue record for this book is
  available from the British Library

  ISBN 1-85389-899-6 pbk

First published in Great Britain by Robert Hale Ltd., 1997

Copyright © 1997 by Vic J. Hanson

Cover illustration © Longaron by arrangement with Norma Editorial S.A.

The right of Vic J. Hanson to be identified as the author of this work has been asserted by him in accordance with the Copyright, Designs and Patents Act, 1988

Published in Large Print 1999 by arrangement with Robert Hale Ltd.

Dales Large Print is an imprint of
Library Magna Books Ltd.
Printed and bound in Great Britain by
T.J. International Ltd., Cornwall, PL28 8RW.

For George and Joan
'Friends of Amos' from way back

PART 1

Chicken Creek
Shake-Up

One

The gunshot resounded as the slug came through the window, bringing slivers of shattered glass, buzzing like an angry hornet, boring into the chest of the man who sat facing the shattered panes. His clawing hands swept his playing cards completely off the table and on to the sawdust-sprinkled floor.

He was driven back and spun half-around by the impact of the bullet and his blood spattered the cards of the man who sat next to him—the tall, lean, moustached one they called Amos.

Amos rose, and already his long-barrelled Dragoon Colt was in his hand. His chair rocked, righted itself, but another chair went completely over as the other two card-players backed awkwardly from the table.

The man who had been hit came off his chair finally and lay flat on his back, his sightless eyes staring upwards at the smoke-wreathed ceiling. A round wash of blood spread slowly across his shirt-front.

Amos, gun lifted, had moved to the door. Drawing their guns also, the other two men followed him.

One of them said, 'I saw nothin' out there.'

There was no more shooting, not much noise at all, only cautious movements behind the three men.

'I'll cover you, Amos,' said the man who had spoken before, and he moved to the window on the other side of the door from the shattered one. The other man reholstered his gun, turned back to the fallen one, got down.

The sun had gone and the shadows were long. The 'keep had lit the lamp behind the bar but no other lights shone. This was the old swamper's job and he was on his knees behind a table. He wasn't the only one who'd taken cover. The barkeep half-crouched behind his bulwark, the snout of his shotgun poking up.

'Take care,' said Amos and he crouched low, butting through the doors.

His back-up man followed him in like fashion, lower even, down on his knees almost, sideways like a lopsided land crab.

Nothing happened. The day had been hot and, even now, there was a sort of furnace breath, no breeze at all. There was no more light out here than there was in the interior of the saloon as the batwings swung gently back and forward.

An old-timer and a younger man stood on the sidewalk on the other side of the street, both gesticulating in the direction of the two men with drawn guns. There wasn't anybody else human in the street and no horse, cat or curdog.

'Watch yourself,' barked Amos.

But the old man came hesitantly across the street.

The younger man, his son, stayed put,

glancing about him quickly. A tow-haired boy showed himself at a corner and the man waved him back and he disappeared. Then the man, the younger one, followed the elder across the street.

The old-timer said, 'We didn't see nothin',' turned on his son, asked, 'Where's Benjy?'

'Just saw him. He's outa the way.'

Benjy, the tow-head boy, was the young man's son, the elder's grandson.

'We didn't even hear a horse,' said the old-timer and the younger man shook his head from side to side.

There was a sort of darkness as if presaging a storm.

'Didn't you see anything at all, Jube?' Amos's companion asked.

'Nope. Neither did Herb; did you, Herb?'

The younger man shook his head again. He had dark saturnine features and might have been called handsome but for a cast in one eye.

His father asked, 'Anybody get shot?'

Amos's companion jerked a thumb backwards. 'Dealey. Plumb through the window and right in the brisket. Dead as a skunk.'

Amos wasn't talking any more, moved away down the street, still with his gun in his hand, the long barrel of the specially modified Dragoon gleaming dully.

He cut across to the opposite sidewalk.

A female head with a mop of iron-grey hair popped from a window and then disappeared again.

A wagon came down the street with timber on it, a young Mexican on the seat behind the two horses. Amos paused. He said something to the boy who shook his sombrero-ed head slowly from side to side.

Amos's companion began to follow him, but taking the opposite side, where folks were coming cautiously through the batwings of the saloon.

Amos turned about, said, 'The boy saw

nothing out there. The shooter must've gone the other way or is still in town.'

The oldster and his son had gone back to the sidewalk on Amos's side of the street and didn't seem to know what to do as Amos passed them. The boy Benjy joined them and they didn't tell him to go.

'I'm with you, Amos,' said the man, moving parallel on the other side of the street.

Amos said, 'All right, Deke.'

Deke said, 'Dealey was no prize package but he was my friend. I don't know who'd want to shoot 'im like that.'

So who, and what the hell were they looking for?

A pudgy young man with a star on his breast accosted them, asked what was going on. They told him. Then Amos said, 'How's Beaky?'

'He's still sick. The doc says he's got to stay in bed.' The bovine-featured deputy wagged his head dolefully up and down. 'We heard the shooting an' he tried to get

16

up. I had to hold him. Then he passed out. I got down here soon as I could.'

'Sure you did,' said Deke. 'Sure you did.' He had a sardonic way of speaking.

'I didn't see anything,' said the deputy lamely.

Deke said, 'A goddam will o' the wisp, huh?'

Amos didn't say anything.

Beaky Teal, so-called because of his huge nose, was the local sheriff. The pudgy deputy was pinch-hitting for him now and not very professionally. Still, this was probably the first killing the boy knew anything about. He couldn't know anything more than Amos and Deke; and they didn't know anything except that Dealey was dead.

A sharpshooter, Amos was thinking, a pro. And this was the first shooting they'd seen in this town for a long time. Beaky Teal, in bed with acute bronchitis—that was what the doc had called it—had been out looking for (allegedly) stolen beef when he'd been caught in a thunderstorm, him and young deputy Lionel, who'd had to tote him home.

The deputy and his two helpers ranged the town looking for a killer, a stranger, anything whatever, and came up with nothing. Then, like history repeating itself, the dark skies opened and the rain deluged. The three men took refuge with the local undertaker who had to be told about the demise of Dealey anyway.

Two

Deputy Lionel said, 'I guess I ought to get a posse together. That's what the chief would do, ain't it?'

Deke said doubtfully, 'I dunno.'

Amos said, 'Where would you take 'em? Huh? Any trail would be washed out by the rain. Anyway, I'm inclined to think the killer is still in town. He did his job and slipped into hiding.'

'I'm agreeing with you, yeh,' said Deke.

'I guess ...' Lionel's voice tailed off. He was a plump, drowned rat, and the other two were little better. The undertaker was dry as a bone and looked as lugubrious as ever. Yesterday he'd buried a ninety-three-year-old half-breed ex-whore called Cherokee Lil. He'd had no business today and that was changed now, but he didn't look any happier than usual.

'Boot Hill will be awash,' he said.

As soon as Sheriff Teal heard the outer door close as his deputy left the front law office the older man got out of bed again. With twilight outside now, his room was dark. He dressed very gingerly as if the sparsely carpeted floor was covered in eggs. He had to rest intermittently, sitting on the edge of the bed, his heart pounding, his chest feeling tight and sore, taking his breath.

The doc had told him not to move. But the doc was an old fart.

Teal couldn't find his boots. He lit the lamp and saw that one boot was to hand, but the other was under the bed. He had to get down on his hands and knees to grope for the limp thing which, however, kept slipping from his grasp like a crouching, living animal determined to elude him.

He finally grabbed it and brought it forth. He was blowing like a norther over the open prairies. He managed to struggle the boots on to his rubbery legs and he sat again.

Stir yourself, you goat, he told himself— you've got to go see what's happening in your town. There had been only one shot, but that was enough. There was an ominous silence now.

He rose and went over to the door and tried it, realizing then that Lionel had locked it after him to keep his ailing chief in, safe, out of harm.

But the chief was unappreciative, cursing, turning, moving over to the window.

That was when he saw the rain begin. And then he saw the figure go across outside, furtively it seemed.

Teal blew out the lamp, unlatched the window, lifted it. He thought he saw the man he had spotted go round a corner. Nothing moved now out there. The window was low. The lawman grabbed his gun rig from where it had been left on a nearby chair. He buckled himself up and felt right and clambered through the window and crossed the beaten earth to the corner.

He turned the corner and saw the man ahead of him. Then he spotted a second man and two horses.

It was the second man, turning away from the horses and looking towards his friend, who spotted the burly, elderly lawman.

'Hold on there, boys,' Teal shouted.

The rain was coming faster.

The man who was nearest to Teal turned and the sheriff saw a lean, dark face, not old, but aged in malice.

A gun, raising. Teal hadn't seen it being drawn. It gleamed dully in the dark and the rain.

Teal reached for his own weapon, knowing as he did so that he was slower than he should have been. And, as if on cue, the rain seemed to lash in sudden fury.

He didn't hear the shot: it was all part

of the greater thing, the thudding in his head and the great blow which propelled him backwards as if his heavy, aching body was that of a gimcrack doll.

He fell on his back and knew he had lost his gun. The rain beat at him as if it would drive him into the ground. There was a vibration under him and he knew that horses were running. But he just wanted to lie there ...

'I swear I heard another shot,' said the deputy, Lionel, who was nearest to the window.

Amos said, 'I didn't hear anything but the rain.'

Deke said, 'Me neither.'

Lionel pointed. 'It seemed to come from that direction. Down by the law office, likely. I think we oughta ...' Then the plump boy was uncertain again.

The cadaverous undertaker had been looking from one to the other of them as they spoke. Maybe he sensed more business. He said, 'If you gents want to go out I have slickers.'

'For Pete's sake,' said Amos. 'Oh, all right.'

'They belonged to corpses but they're quite respectable.'

'Well, the corpses won't need them any more I guess.'

'All right, suh.' The corpse-man turned, opened a tall cabinet that looked not unlike an upended coffin and brought forth the long garments. The trio picked one apiece. Deke and Lionel were both stocky and were outfitted right champion. But Amos's slicker was tight and didn't cover his knees. It would keep his gun dry though, and maybe that was all that mattered.

The three pulled their hats down and went out into the rain and turned in the direction of the jailhouse. They kept in the shelter of overhangs as much as they could, clattering along the boardwalk as the driving rain sought them out.

They reached their destination and

Lionel said, 'I locked Beaky in his room. I better go see ...'

Amos said, 'We'll go round back.' He was a hunter. He was very wet, his knees sticking to his pants. But he was out now; he was hunting; he meant to do the job properly, even if it turned out he was chasing the proverbial wild goose. And it'd be pretty bedraggled at that.

Lionel unlocked the office door, closed it behind him, went through. He would have to unlock the bedroom door after passing through the comfortable little sitting-room.

Sheriff Teal was a widower with one son who was in school at a neighbouring town which had better learning facilities. He came home each weekend on the stagecoach.

A door at the deputy's left led into the kitchen. The cell-block was back off the office, angling off near the sitting-room door.

The door of the sheriff's bedroom was

on the other side of the sitting-room opposite where Lionel had entered, a straight walk through without having to skirt any furniture.

There was a window in the sitting-room which let in good light. Lionel saw Amos and Deke pass by outside as he crossed the room, hastening his steps. He was surprised that Sheriff Beaky hadn't heard him and yelled out, bad-temperedly. Maybe the chief—and Lionel was fond of the man—was asleep. Yeh, and maybe he was just being awkward, playing possum.

Maybe he was worse!

Lionel fumbled the keys, almost dropped them, managed to get the right one, inserted it in the lock, turned it, pushed the door open.

There was no sound, no voice. Then the deputy saw that the bed was empty, the clothes tumbled.

There was a draught from the wide-open window, and the rain, fiercer than ever now it seemed, lashed in gustily.

The deputy went over to the window and bent and peered out. Through the veil of rain he saw that Amos and Deke were bending over something which lay in the mud. Deke turned, saw Lionel, beckoned to him.

The deputy climbed through the window. He heard Amos say, 'He's talkin'.' And then the tall man was down on one knee in the mud and bending over the huddled form of Sheriff Beaky Teal.

As the deputy reached the two men Amos rose, his pants' leg dripping wet. He said, 'He's gone. Shot plumb centre in the chest. It's a wonder he lasted this long. As if he was waiting for us.'

'So I did hear a shot,' said Lionel dully. The rain ran down his face like tears.

Deke said, 'He mumbled words. What did he say?'

Amos said, 'I only caught a bit. He said "rowel". Rowel. That was the only plain thing.'

'That's the wheels on spurs,' said Deke.

'The sharp 'uns mainly I guess. Fancy. Mexicans like 'em. I wouldn't use one o' them sort on any cayuse o' mine.'

Amos said, 'Yeh, that's what Beaky meant I reckon. His killer was wearin' spurs with spikes on 'em.'

Lionel hadn't joined in this discussion. 'Let's get 'im inside,' he said, bending over his old chief. The other two hastened to help.

Three

Colehan and Billy T rode with their heads down against the rain, their slouch hats pulled low. They rode close together like they mostly did, as if they were scared of losing each other, though neither of them were scared of anything much.

Billy T was called so because his last name was well-nigh unpronounceable. As far as Billy knew—and they'd been together quite a while now—Colehan had always been just Colehan; that was what Billy called him, and so did everybody else it seemed.

They were pushing their horses a mite through the rain which didn't seem as if it were aiming to quit, though maybe it wasn't coming now with quite so much fury.

After a job, Billy T—who was the front-man—always liked to talk. He leaned his head towards his partner and shouted, 'I didn't figure for that ol' goat coming through that window like that.'

'He didn't see much of us,' said Colehan.

'He ain't about to see any more either. I reckon I got him good.'

'Yeh. So now mebbe we pick up the rest of the *dinero,* huh? But that's a long spell o' riding yet an' this ain't the night for ridin'. So where do we go first?'

'Call on the twins. Nobody will look for us there. And the twins don't talk.'

'They better not,' said Colehan darkly.

But Billy T didn't hear him now, was pushing his horse forward. Talking after the kill was good, a smile, a relaxation. But having a woman was even better, and the twins were prime womenfolk.

Billy veered his horse off the narrow trail, which any posse would be following he figured, and cut across the grass.

Colehan followed him, knowing this was the shortest way to the Caracterus twins' smallholding out there on the flat prairies where in daylight you could gaze over acres of unbroken land. In the other direction, at the end of the narrow trail which petered out here and there, were hills, and likely any posse would figure for the two boys to be holing up there.

Billy was mighty smart, Colehan had to give him that; and, for all his gab, he was nervelessly professional also and they had a good thing going between them. Colehan, the big quiet man who looked like a working ranny. And Billy T, the dark-featured fancy boy with wicked eyes and a ready smile, the charm of a sidewinder drowsing in the sun—when he wasn't talking a blue streak; and mostly that charmed the lasses and lads also.

Colehan, though Irish, wasn't adept at the blarney. He didn't rightly know what Billy was: in that direction the fancy boy could be as close-mouthed as a wild bronc with a muzzle on his nose.

The rain seemed to be abating.

Gracie said, 'Goddamn you—you've still got your boots and spurs on.' She buffeted him with her knees and her lusty thighs, pushed him with her hands.

He rolled off her and hit the edge of the bed and slid from there to the floor where he rolled, laughing hysterically.

'Damn your hide,' screamed Gracie. 'You poked me with them spikes.'

Still laughing, Billy T was trying to get up, got halfway. Then he tripped over his pants, which were still around his ankles, and went down again.

Gracie leaned out of bed, her naked bubs dangling, and began to beat him on the head with her fists. She overbalanced and fell on top of him and they rolled in a tangle of arms and legs, Billy laughing, Gracie screaming. But her noise turned to laughter too, and she straddled him, sitting on his chest well away from the wicked spiked rowels.

'You scratched my legs, damn you,' she said.

'You got some salve, haven't you, baby? I'll put some o' that on for you.'

'Not till you get all them duds off, jackass.'

'That's me. The jackass. Get off'n me, woman.'

She moved to the edge of the bed and watched him while he divested himself of everything remaining on his lean muscular carcass, including his boots and spurs. She had a fine figure herself and she sat there to tease him.

She saw that he was ready for her again and she leaned back, revealing herself even more, and twisted and reached her arm out to the cabinet at the other side of the bed and slid out the small drawer at the top and delved, her body parts rippling, and dug out the round box of salve she kept for small hurts. She and her twin

Sadie worked hard on their smallholding (when they weren't entertaining 'gentlemen friends' like Billy T and Colehan) and often got knocks and scratches.

Once Gracie had gotten a nasty cut in her back from falling on to their small ploughshare. As per coincidence, Billy T had happened along at that time, and the lean boy had fixed Gracie's hurts. A man of strange pursuits which Gracie didn't want to know about, he had been surprisingly gentle.

He was the same now, though he said her scratches were mere flea-bits. The doctoring became a tussle and both of them became daubed with the salve which was bright yellow in colour, and Billy said it smelled like horse piss. Gracie said, yeh, mebbe that was one of its ingredients and it was a concoction of her own mixed with her own fair hand. Billy said she was a lying bitch, but 'purty' with it, and he pinned her to the bed.

In the room next door Sadie and Colehan

were sitting up in bed, smoking long black cheroots which were the girls' favourites. They were so alike in so many things, and if they dressed alike many folks couldn't tell 'em apart.

Colehan and Billy T, who did turn about with the two of them, had got them sorted out now, agreeing that Gracie was the most feisty. Colehan liked Sadie best, however, because she was the quietest.

The big Irishman puffed, wreathing his head in smoke, and said, 'Why do them two have to be so tarnation noisy?'

Sadie said, 'They're quiet now.' She stubbed out the end of her cheroot and turned to him and caressed the matt of black hair on his broad chest. She was built like her sister, her breasts twin globes.

She said, 'You're taking a long time over that smoke.'

Colehan said, 'I'm finished, I'm finished,' and stubbed out the black weed.

'Oh, no, buster, you ain't finished yet,' whispered the girl.

The two boys rode off in the early morning in a world that sparkled after the rain. They were out of sight of the smallholding when Colehan said, 'What happened to them big spurs of yours?'

'Gracie took 'em as a souvenir. I'll get some more when we hit a town. I don't need 'em with this cayuse anyway. He's as champion as a hound-dog, ain't you, boy?' Billy T patted the horse's neck and the beast snorted softly.

He had come into town one day behind two trotting horses and with the small wagon behind piled with his goods and his wife and daughter on the high seat with him. Some folks had recognized him from time back, though nobody there had known him at all well.

His name was Amos. He liked to be called just Amos.

He came from Golden Bluffs, him and the two females; he'd been marshal there, had cleaned that town pretty good as folks eventually learned.

He wasn't a lawman now. He'd heard that the armoury shop was up for sale after the death of its owner. He did a deal with the late owner's family and moved in there with his family. He was a man who knew about all kinds of weapons, there was no denying that.

Folks learned that though Amos and the woman—a mighty pretty female called Stella—were married, the daughter wasn't Amos's. She was called Molly and was as pretty as her mother.

The town of Chicken Creek where Amos now had his business was smaller and quieter than Golden Bluffs where he had toted a star.

That is, until a gambler called Dealey got bushwhacked—and Amos and other gamblers could easily have stopped a bullet too—and the killer had disappeared as if the earth or skies had swallowed him.

'A professional job,' Amos had been heard to say, and he was a man who knew about such things.

Dealey had been more than somewhat of a pain in the ass. But who would want to kill him or get him killed?

It seemed pretty certain that two men had been involved, though maybe only one had done the shooting, the other standing watch with the horses. It seemed certain also that only one man had spotted them and that had been Sheriff Teal and he had been shot down like a dog. Ol' Beaky had been popular and most folks were more incensed about his useless death than they were about the summary execution of Dealey.

Dealey the Dealer he had gotten to be called and some disgruntled losers had murmured that he cheated. But Dealey hadn't seemed an aggressive man, except with a hand of poker; had never used a gun in Chicken Creek in the year and an odd few days he'd been there after riding in out of the sun, a loner on a rawboned grey stallion that had outlived him.

Amos had been heard to say 'That was the best damn hand I had in all that time.' He had picked up the bloodstained cards and put them on the sill beneath the broken window.

The old saloon swamper, who was somewhat of a handyman also had mended the window and the bloody pasteboards had disappeared. The oldster was a sort of picker up of trifles to peddle on the side to replenish his meagre income. Maybe he'd sell the 'death cards' to some passing souvenir collector at a later date.

Nobody was playing cards now and a couple of funerals were being planned.

Four

She was a slim, dark, lovely woman with big brown eyes, even white teeth, a ready smile, and a sometimes ribald sense of humour. Her name was Stella and he had known her a long time. Her first husband, before he was killed at the end of a gun, had been Amos's deputy and his good friend. That seemed such a long time ago.

He had watched Stella's daughter, Molly, grow up: she had called him 'Uncle Amos'. A slim dark beauty, still at school, she would grow up to be a lovely young lady with her mom's warm nature and sense of humour: Amos knew this.

He sat with them at the breakfast table and it seemed to him that he would never want to leave. But he knew that he would have to. He knew that he didn't really have to explain this to Stella. But he figured he had to do that as well. She knew so much already.

She hadn't known much about the cardsharp called Dealey the Dealer, but Sheriff Beaky Teal had been her friend, a bluff genial man with a mischievous humour who had made her and Molly laugh, sitting here at this very table, sometimes with Amos, sometimes without him, and drinking her prime coffee and wolfing her hot cakes.

'I'm the one,' Amos said. 'I fit in. And ol' Beaky was valuable to us.'

'I know, honey.'

He knew, too, that Stella had nursed Beaky in his sickness. Pity Beaky hadn't stayed in bed like he'd been told to do. But there was no use in dwelling on that now.

'Pity about that rain,' Amos murmured as if talking to himself.

But this morning was bright and sparkling. A dry, warming morning. But not a happy one.

'How about the funerals?' Stella asked tentatively.

'The undertaker has facilities ... If we don't get back Beaky will understand ... *Would* understand.' Amos was becoming faltering in manner and speech, and that was unusual for him.

Stella knew that he was raring to go. His friend, a lawman, had been killed and he, Amos, was lawman again now, a hunter. She had hoped this would never happen again. But she would never have dreamed of telling him this.

'Take care, my love,' she said softly.

He bent and kissed her. Then he turned and kissed Molly. She clung to him momentarily, her dark, curly head bent to hide tears, not saying anything at all.

Mischievously, she had started to call him 'Pop'; privately, to her mother, Amos had confessed that he was sometimes beginning to feel like a budding mossyhorn and the dark, lovely woman had riposted with 'That you are, bucko, that you are'.

He never put on his gun gear with the women watching him. He kept it upstairs. He went up, and he strapped it on. He did not have to go into the kitchen again and he did not call.

He went through the shadowed shop, looking around him as if it were for the first time. A congenial place. A place of magic in the half-light with bars of sunlight coming through the wide window. There were weapons and accessories all around him. On shelves and hanging on the wall, and even festooning parts of the ceiling.

He had himself renamed the place The Armoury, considering it fitting. The previous owner had been some sort of a connoisseur of warlike gadgets and shields and emblems, had a collection of bullet-proof vests of leather or hide lined with steel, a steel breastplate which had belonged to a murderous individual called Pecos Charlie; Indian lances and strange amulets that were supposed to deflect bullets or knives—all kinds of knives and cutting instruments, lots of them; war hatchets, blunderbusses, carbines, muskets, military flags ... Looking at it again as if for the first time, Amos wondered, as he must do, whether it would be for the last time. So many times in so many towns! Thinking this and then pushing it to the back of his mind and getting on with the job which had to be done.

He hadn't opened the shop yet this morning. He shot the bolts, turned the key, lifted the latch. He opened the heavy door and the sun streamed in at him.

Stella would be out soon, would look after things. He strode down to the smart livery stable where he kept his horse. Right now he was having a small stable built out back of the shop.

He had been sworn in by the local judge and was now honorary marshal of Chicken Creek until a new sheriff or constable could be sent for. He had a star but hadn't pinned it on: it was in the top pocket of his leather vest.

He strode down the middle of a quiet street as he had done so many times before in so many streets and the years rolled behind him and his shadow marched before him in the sunlight.

His two deputies were already waiting. Deke and Lionel. He had turned down a posse. After the rain there'd be no trail anyway. And a bunch of irate townies might be hindrance rather than help.

Amos could track, had had plenty of practice. He figured that he might pick up some tracks or signs on harder ground out towards the hills where the ground was rockier and the torrential rain hadn't turned it into mud.

Thing was, though, if the two miscreants were professionals at what they did they mightn't try the hills at all, figuring that that was just what pursuers might expect them to do—they might veer off the trail before that. Time would tell. 'Let's go,' he said brusquely—and the three of them mounted up.

As they rode Deke told Amos—with interpolations from Deputy Lionel—all he knew about the murdered man called Dealey, whom Amos had only known as a poker-playing opponent to be carefully watched. Dealey had been no pantywaist though, no show-off, and Amos hadn't had any firm opinions about the man at all. He didn't know a hell of a lot about this young man called Deke, either, only that he was strong, fast, forthright, probably a good sidekick to have in a pinch.

Deke was well-built, handsome in a ruddy sort of a way, handled himself better than the pudgy, clumsy Lionel. But Amos didn't sell the latter short, wasn't averse to having him along: maybe he'd prove to have hidden depths or something. Anyway, he couldn't possibly be a no-go character or the shrewd Beaky Teal wouldn't have stood him for deputy as long as he had.

Beaky had been Lionel's friend and mentor and the young man still grieved for him and, in fact, had more right to be on this vengeance trail than Amos or Deke had. He followed tamely in the wake of the new honorary marshal, the—to him—elderly and fabled hunter, gunfighter, killer.

He joined in the conversation with Deke, the subject being the late, if not wholly lamented, Dealey the Dealer. But Lionel didn't seem to know much more about Dealey than Amos did and both of them left the straight talking to Deke, with Amos asking a question from time to time.

Five

'I saw somebody, Dad,' said the boy called Benjy. 'A stranger.'

'Goldarn it, boy, why didn't you tell us this before,' said his father, Herb.

Just then Herb's father came into the kitchen. The three of them had been in Chicken Creek when Dealey the Dealer and Sheriff Beaky Teal had been murdered. They had, in fact, been the only folk nearby when Amos and Deke had come running out of the saloon after Dealey's murder.

'He saw somebody when we were in town,' said Herb. And then the old man asked his grandson pretty much the same question that the father had done.

The boy was forthright, blue-eyed, towheaded. He said, 'I guess I was kind of scared. Anyway, the man wasn't carrying a gun and he seemed harmless. There was only me and him around and you two were ahead of me and just round a corner out of sight.'

'But was it after the shooting?'

'Ye-eh. I guess.'

'Did the man take notice of you?'

'He didn't seem to see me.'

'What did he look like?'

'About your build, Dad, but younger I guess. Lean and dark. But he was moving quickly ...'

'Runnin' away?' said old Jube.

'No, just hurrying, I thought, as if he'd got to meet somebody.'

'Way it went, poor ol' Beakey an' all, he'd likely meet somebody I guess.'

'Maybe ...' the boy began; then tailed off. It didn't do to argue with grown-ups if they seemed to have made their minds up about something.

'Get on with your chores,' his father told him, and he wandered out of the kitchen. His mother was feeding the chickens. She called out, 'You going to finish chopping that wood?'

'Yes, Ma.' He went to the woodpile, the stubby logs, picked up the long-handled axe. He got going with something he liked doing. The axe sang; and *thwacked* satisfyingly. Like the rest of his family he was sturdy, healthy.

They had a small ranch, a comfortable spread in near sight of the hills when the air was good. Plenty of grazing ground around for cattle and horses, no rocks till further on at the foothills.

They had two hands, both young, though not as young as Benjy. A Mexican vaquero and a half-breed who had some Apache in him but was completely reliable: he was Benjy's special friend. The two were out now hunting for strays, not a lengthy or hard task most times as the stock didn't wander on to the wild land in the foothills where the ground had no sustenance except for the cholla that grew profusely there, twisted like a nightmare, bitter as a sidewinder's tongue.

Billy T and Colehan were going good in the sunshine when the latter's horse was bitten by something and its legs went from under it. The beast pitched forward violently as if in a paroxysm, throwing its rider over its head. Colehan came down heavily on his right shoulder and shouted with pain but managed to scramble out of the path of the falling horse which rolled, twitched, became still with its teeth bared, its eyes turned upward milkily.

If there had been a rattlesnake he had moved like greased lightning and was nowhere to be seen in the grass which had been cropped by livestock and wasn't long.

Maybe it had been a poisonous spider or even some flying thing. Done was done anyway, and the horse was dead, and Colehan was cussing like a muleskinner as he struggled to rise to his feet. He made it but was kind of lopsided, clutching his shoulder.

'I think it's busted,' he said.

Billy T slid down from the saddle but didn't seem to know what to do next, which was unusual for him.

'There're some riders coming,' said Colehan, his broad face twisted with pain.

Billy turned, saw the two riders, said, 'I hope they're harmless. If they are we'll ask for their help.'

They were two younkers, a Mexican and a slimmer younger boy who, though togged like a working ranny, looked half-Indian.

Billy T indicated the dead horse and his sweating partner who looked as if he was about to pass out at any moment.

Billy said, 'We're in a tight, friends.'

The Mexican boy said, 'We weel he'p you.'

The brown-skinned boy didn't say anything, just nodded and smiled.

Deke said, 'Dealey was a dab hand with the cards. I know some losers said he'd been cheating, but they didn't say that to his face. He was quiet, affable man. But there was something about him ...'

'A damn' mystery man,' put in Deputy Lionel.

'I think he was just slick with his hands, his eyes. The way he handled himself. A poker face when needed, and maybe he was running a long lucky streak.'

Lionel said, 'It seemed to have lasted since he'd been in Chicken Creek.'

'Yeh, he seemed to make his way well with the cards, though he did do some waddying in between—he was great hand at the last big roundup and he was good.'

'You were there, Deke?' said Amos.

'Sure. That's what I do, ain't it? I ain't much different than Dealey was, but nobody's tried to shoot me yet, have they?'

Lionel said, 'You're too ornery to get shot.' The two deputies seemed to like each other, and honorary marshal Amos was glad of that.

'Deke said, 'I never heard about Dealey before he came to Chicken Creek. He was always kinda well-dressed, and he had a fine gun-rig. I never saw him use it, though.'

Amos said, 'A man doesn't have to show off 'less he's pushed.' He seemed to be speaking absently, was leaning, looking past his horse's neck, watching the ground. The trail was narrow, intermittent, had actually petered out a few times. Now the ground each side of it was becoming scrubby and brown.

Amos said, 'Hold hard, *amigos,*' and he dismounted and went down on one knee, inspecting the ground, looking forward and to left and right.

'I figure they moved off here and headed that way.' He pointed with a gloved hand.

Lionel said 'What's out there?'

Deke didn't say anything, looking about him, seemed to be cogitating. He got down from his horse and joined Amos who had raised himself upwards to his lean full length. They looked out at flat land, a long expanse disappearing into the heat haze.

Suddenly Deke chortled and slapped his hand down hard on his knee, said, 'Yeh. *Yeh!* I know somep'n that's out there. Gracie and Sadie, the Caracterus twins.'

Lionel said, 'I heard of them. But I've never seen 'em.'

Amos said, 'I've never heard of them. Do you think ... ?' He looked at Deke who said, 'I wonder.'

Lionel had not dismounted. The other two climbed into their saddles again. Amos said, 'Let's take a look out there.' He led the way. Then Deke caught up with him, guiding him. Lionel, a somewhat bemused look on his pudgy face, brought up the rear.

Six

As they saw the buildings dimly shimmering in the heat-haze Amos halted them and got down from his horse once more.

Deke and Lionel waited, looking down at the ground, following the older man's eyes as he got down on one knee and peered. They had come to realize that the new marshal was a pretty good tracker as well as a gunfighter and a fair to middling hand with the colourful pasteboards.

'Riders certainly came this way,' Deke said, not to be outdone it seemed.

'You're right there, bucko,' said Amos, turning his head, a thin smile on his lean moustached face with the curious slatey, bluey-grey eyes. 'And they were making for that little spread, whatever it is.'

'That's where the girls hang out,' said

Deke as Amos mounted up again.

Lionel didn't say anything, seemed somehow as if he were strangely ill at ease.

The cluster of buildings became clearer. 'Watch yourselves,' said Amos caustically. 'The girls might have company.'

'They might at that,' said Deke, grinning. But then each man eased himself lower in the saddle.

Then they all saw the girls, though, standing out on the dirt yard staring at them.

One of the girls had a rifle half-lifted in her hands, and Deke said, 'Damned if I can tell 'em apart, particularly at this distance.'

As they got still nearer the girl with the long gun lowered it but didn't ground it. The other one shaded her eyes with her hand. She called, 'Well, hello there, Deke.'

'Hi-yuh, girls,' said Deke who obviously still couldn't tell one of 'em from the other.

Amos had pinned his star on his chest. It had belonged to Beaky Teal who didn't need it any more. It was gleaming and prominent but not inscribed. Constable, marshal, deputy, dog-catcher, sheriff. a star was a badge of authority: folks took note of a badge.

The girls backed off. The one with the gun sloped it and even said, 'Welcome'. they led the way into the house. Deke had got them spotted by now. 'You weren't gonna shoot anybody were you, Gracie?' he said to the one with the gun who was dressed pretty much like her sister except for a bright red bandanna round her neck.

'Hell, no,' said Gracie, the feisty one.

She put her gun in a corner of the cluttered living-room.

'We're out on law business,' said Amos. He looked from one to the other of his two deputies and added,

'Search the place. But do it carefully.'

'You can't do that,' said Gracie, but

without any great vehemence, halting even, not even glancing now at the rifle in the corner.

There was something intimidating—and completely uncompromising about this tall man with the cold eyes who looked at her as if she were a snake in a cage. She didn't return that gaze with the bold look she had.

'I'll go make coffee,' said the other girl. No introductions had been exchanged.

Gracie sat down on a chair by a cluttered little table from which a brightly knitted woollen swathe spilled, a covering of some kind. Gracie pointed a finger at the door through which her sister had disappeared. 'My twin is called Sadie,' she said. 'I'm Gracie.' She pointed at the colourful pile on the table. 'Sadie did that. She's kinda clever wouldn't you say?'

'I would.' The man had a deep voice, sounded like a native Texican. 'I heard Deke call you Gracie,' he added and sat down on a chair facing her; asked, 'You had any visitors lately, missy?'

'Not so's you'd notice. But Deke's an old friend. He's welcome any time.'

'We followed tracks leading here.'

'I don't think ...' She forgot what she was about to say and her voice tailed off. Her gaze was intermittent; she lowered it. That man's eyes seemed to be coldly searing her heart and mind, reading them.

Sadie came in with the coffee. She had been quick. But Deke and Lionel were right on her heels and Deke had a pair of wickedly spiked spurs dangling in his fingers, and said, 'Look what I found, Amos.'

Amos took them, examined them. Sadie bustled with a steaming jug with mugs. Amos held up the spurs, looked at Gracie, asked, 'How long you had these?'

She shrugged. 'Souvenirs.'

'All right. Who gave 'em to you?'

'A gentleman friend.'

'Which gentleman friend?' cut in Deke. He had found a seat, a chair. Lionel was sitting on a stool in a corner like a naughty schoolboy.

Gracie said, 'You know I don't talk about my gentlemen friends, Deke. Neither of us do. Ain't that right, Sadie?'

'Sure is.' Sadie poured coffee.

Amos said, 'You're going to talk about this one. He came here yesterday, didn't he? Him and his pard.'

'I don't know who you're talking about.'

'Me neither,' said Sadie, handing coffee around for which the three gentlemen thanked her politely.

Amos said, 'You're going to tell us who those two are. We are going to stay here till you do no matter how long it takes. Those two boys could've been involved in two murders back in Chicken Creek.'

'Who ...?'

They told her.

And then Sadie said, 'Dealey. We knew him. And that sheriff was a nice man. We've got to tell them, Gracie.'

So they did. And Deke said, 'Billy T! A goddamn hired gun.'

'I heard of him,' said Amos. And Lionel, from his corner, said, 'I think I did. I think Sheriff Teal mentioned him once.'

Sadie was looking at the plump deputy on his stool, and now she said, 'I know you. We've seen you before. A kind of deputy. Your name's Lionel.'

Lionel went as red as his bovine, weatherbeaten features would allow. He had told his two companions earlier, back on the trail, that he'd never seen the twins.

But Amos couldn't be bothered with that, asked, 'When did those two leave an' which way did they go?'

'Away from the hills,' said Gracie. 'Maybe around 'em. Don't know.'

'No,' said Sadie.

'We'll pick up the trail again,' said Amos grimly. He swallowed his coffee and rose.

The big man with the busted shoulder was in the tiny room upstairs with the narrow bunk. Old Jube had said that the feller, whom he'd bandaged, strapped, seen to as best he could, should have a proper sawbones as soon as possible or he was going to lose his fin or become crippled for life; or even get gangrene or something, and that could be the finish of him.

Young Benjy joined his grandfather and his mother in the kitchen, his eyes as round as small saucers.

'The fancy one in there sitting with Dad,' he jerked a thumb in the direction of the next-door sitting-room, 'he's the one I saw in town after the shootin' at the saloon.'

The woman gave a shocked exclamation. Old Jube raised a finger to his lips. 'You sure?'

'I'm certain sure.'

'Stay here, both o' you.'

There was a smaller door, leading to

the passage and the stairs, hat-rack at the bottom, a cabinet half-hidden behind it. Jube delved into the cabinet and brought forth a Bulldog pistol, stubby, wicked-looking. He tucked it into his belt and hid it beneath the floppy woollen vest he invariably wore. He entered the sitting-room through the other wider door.

'The fancy one' was sitting with Jube's son, Herb, but he rose as the old man entered, and he said, 'I was just saying I ought to be goin'. My partner will understand. He knows we were on our way to important business and are now long overdue. I'm sure I can leave him in the hands of you good folks and you will see he gets doctored properly.'

A polite young cuss who sounds genuine, Jube thought, but now something a mite too hasty about him maybe: I've got to find some way to keep him here. He might be a sort of innocent bystander, but I've got to know for sure.

He said, 'My daughter-in-law's fixing a

meal. We thought you were going to stay a while.'

'Thankee, but it can't be done,' the young man said, and he began to walk.

Seven

'Hold on, son,' said Jube. 'You ain't goin' any place yet. Turn around.'

Billy T revolved slowly and faced the dangerous stub-muzzle of Jube's chunky little Bulldog.

'What's going on?' asked Herb, who wasn't quick on the uptake.

'I might ask you the same question, old man,' said the young visitor.

'I want to ask *you* some questions,' said Jube. 'First off, shuck your gunbelt.'

He wasn't an owlhooter, never had been. Had fought in the war. But that had been a different thing: he'd been fighting for what he'd believed in, thought he had, wasn't so sure now. Since then, he'd been a mighty peaceable man, working on the land and with the livestock. He still limped a little with a war wound he had gotten in his left leg.

He hadn't told the young man just how he was required to remove his hardware. He wore his gun on the righthand side, low, tied to his thigh with a whangstring, the gunfighter's way. This main weapon was a later Colt Army .44 with the trigger cut off. It had a formidable hammer and Billy was adept with this.

However, he also had, in a hide sheath in back of his belt, a smaller Colt, a 'Lightning', modified, with a cut-down barrel.

Billy unbuckled his belt with both hands, 'I don't know what this is all about, old man, but I guess I'll have to humour you or you might blow me in half with that leetle gidget of yours.' A handsome smooth-talking young gent; and Herb gazing from him to the old man and back again, not moving, but still looking as if his mis-matched eyes were deceiving him.

Billy had the gunbelt off. He said, 'This hogleg's hair-trigger so I'm gonna lower this gear gently.'

He was taking his time and both Herb and Jube were watching him now as if fascinated, the latter's pistol-muzzle lowered a mite as if, also, he wasn't now quite sure he was doing the right thing.

As he lowered the gunbelt, the young fancy man bent a little. He let the hardware go but, as he rose, he had the smaller back-up Colt in his fist.

As the rest of the gear nudged the floor the gun went off with an impact that matched its nickname, sounding like a cannon-shot in the room, with shocking violence.

The slug from the short-barrelled gun slammed Jube full in his scrawny chest, knocking him backwards as if he'd been standing too near to a cannon and it had recoiled upon him. His finger closed involuntarily on the trigger of his Bulldog pistol and it boomed, a surprising sound from the stubby, blued weapon.

The room was full of gunsmoke and the acrid stink of powder. Herb moved like a turkey avoiding the chop. He had no weapon; he was aimless.

His father, eyes turning up in death, had hit the door-jamb and was sliding down on it, his pistol lying uselessly on the floor—Jube's feet kicking it in his last threshing movements before he became still with only his grey head against the door.

The slug from his pistol, however, had bored into the muscle of Billy T's right arm and his short-nosed back-up gun had fallen to the floor, his blood dripping upon it.

Billy got down on one knee and, with his left hand, gripped the butt of the longer gun in its holster on the rig and yanked it free. That was when Herb, with an inarticulate cry, flung himself at the wounded man.

Billy swung the pistol: a backhanded swipe and the barrel catching Herb on the temple with a dull, metallic *thunk*.

Herb was spun backwards. He sprawled, a lean tangle of arms and legs, and became still.

Herb's missus came to the communicating door from the kitchen with a large, carving knife in her hand. The staring face of young Benjy appeared behind her, eyes bulging, not yet fully comprehending.

The woman almost fell over her father-in-law's body.

Left-handed, Billy fired the Colt .44. It bucked and flamed. The knife spun from the woman's hand and fell across the body of the old man.

She staggered, screamed, 'Benjy, run!' The boy disappeared. Billy, who was losing blood badly, went the other way, through the front door, his left hand clasped to his wound.

He realized he'd left his horse out back and he ran around the house. He expected to see the boy running. But the boy was nowhere in sight.

Billy was getting weak. He reached his horse and climbed into the saddle.

Colehan's horse was nearby. Billy thought vaguely that the big man with the busted shoulder might need it so he left it there. Colehan would have to look after himself.

Billy drove his heels into his mount's flanks. He hadn't gotten himself any new spurs yet. The thought seemed to amuse him and he began to shake in the saddle as the horse sped away.

Next thing he remembered—and he wasn't laughing any more—he was clinging to the horse's neck, was being carried in a dream, a nightmare. Who would've dreamed that a pill in the arm could serve a man so badly.

Colehan heard the shooting, and then the hoofbeats. He rolled out of bed in his long-johns, strapped and bandaged like an Egyptian mummy he had once seen

72

in a fit-up travellin' show. At least, it was supposed to be a mummy.

He lurched to his feet and, in a wobbling rush, made it to the window and peered out. He saw Billy T riding like all hell was on his tail.

Goddam, he's left me, Colehan thought, *goddam him!*

His head began to swim. He crawled back to bed and heaved himself upon it.

In panic, Benjy had run as his ma had told him to run. He had rolled into a ditch where straw was spread for fodder. It was dry and soft.

He had lain as the galloping horse passed, seeing the beast's belly as he jumped, heard the man cursing, urging his mount on, but pain in his voice also.

But there'd been other images in the boy's mind. His grandfather lying still. His father lying still.

Although his ma had been able to speak to him, scream at him even, he had seen her fall, knew she had been hurt.

He didn't know how badly any of them had been hurt.

He had ducked low as he saw the big man appear at the bedroom window. The man had disappeared again ...

Benjy moved out of his concealment and towards the house.

The bedroom window was empty. Even the house looked empty.

He started to trot back to the house. His feet began to drag. He was still scared, apprehensive ...

Eight

Billy T came to his senses, but he was weak, his sight shimmering, though the sun wasn't so bright as it had been.

His shirt on the right-hand side was saturated with blood, his arm hung limply like a blood-soaked dead thing.

He had had wounds before, worse than this, which, though bad, hadn't been in a particularly vulnerable position. How could it have served him so?

But it had.

He shouldn't have passed out! He should have fixed a tourniquet on the arm!

He leaned on the horse's neck again. He was so weak, couldn't seem to stir himself to do anything.

He looked ahead of him, his cheek against the warmth of the horse's neck. He thought he saw buildings. Was salvation there, or would he walk into another bullet, the finish of him?

He had lost a lot of blood. Like a robot, slow, halting, not working very well, the pain grinding into him, he took the bandanna from his neck and did the best he could with it. He used one hand and his teeth, the blood salty on his lips, the pain searing him as he used his last remaining strength to tighten the thin bandage and staunch the blood.

The horse's hooves hit hard ground and the buildings were right in front of him and the man recognized them.

The damn' stupid cayuse had brought him back to where he'd been before.

The twins came out. They were lusty females who soon got him down from his bloodstained saddle and carried him into the house and laid him down.

Their earlier visitors had gone. Not making for the hills, planning to skirt them, if they didn't spot their quarry before.

Going that way, they might even have caught up with Billy T and his partner, Colehan. That is, if the big Irishman hadn't had that unfortunate accident and the two partners hadn't changed their route accordingly and run into more trouble.

So Billy T and Amos and his two deputies had passed each other by a few country miles, going in opposite directions.

Who would have thought that Billy T (wounded to boot) would backtrack—or his horse, remembering he had gotten good sustenance at the hands of the two nice ladies, had decided to do this for him?

Marshal Amos, had he known all the circumstances—and he was not a great believer in coincidence—might have suggested that the malicious fates had taken a hand. The little devil-beings that nobody ever saw or heard, or even *sensed*. He had known an old Mexican who called them 'the devil's children'.

Being Irish, the man called Colehan might have thought of them as being something to do with 'the little people'. But Colehan didn't now know much about anything, except that there had been shooting in the rooms beneath his bedroom, that terrible things had probably happened, and that Billy T had run out on him.

For the second time Colehan dragged himself out of his bed. He managed to lift his gun-rig from a nearby chair but couldn't manage to strap it round his waist. He carried it as he went out through the bedroom door on to the landing.

The man Colehan had heard called Herb was at the bottom of the stairs looking up at him.

The man had blood on his face and a gun in his hand. His squinty eyes were wild in his dark face, tortured, as he raised the gun and pointed it at the big man at the top of the stairs.

The slug hit Colehan in the belly and he smelled the smoke and his own blood and the explosion seem to echo in his brain as he was knocked backwards, hit the jamb of the half-open door behind him and slid around and fell in a heap in the bedroom.

His fallen gun-rig clattered down the stairs and, dull-eyed, Herb picked it up and turned like a thing in a dream, would have disappeared from Colehan's sight had Colehan still been at the top of the stairs. But Colehan wasn't interested any more.

Amos had been tracking. He was a good tracker. He found the place where Colehan had been pitched from his horse and he veered and his two deputies and he went on from there.

They saw the buildings in the distance and Deke said, 'That's Herb Kyle's place.'

Then they saw the riderless horse which, when Deke whistled him, came forward tentatively.

He let them lead him.

They all heard the single shot.

Amos said, 'Spread out. Keep low. Now

c'mon.' He set his horse at a gallop. Lionel and Deke were soon close behind. The riderless horse joined in the game, his mane streaming in the wind.

They slowed down when they saw the boy called Benjy out on the sod in front of the main building. He was waving, his movements frantic, ungainly.

When they came up to him he just stared at them, big-eyed, his mouth working slowly without sound, the tears rolling down his cheeks.

He turned about abruptly and led them to the house.

Old Jube was dead, laid on the couch in the sitting-room. Herb stood bemusedly in the middle of the floor with a gun dangling in his hand. There was a swelling cut on his temple where Billy T's swinging gun had struck him, temporarily stunning him.

Mrs Kyle had been mighty lucky. The bullet from Billy's smaller gun had 'creased' her brow: there was a red mark seared there. She had been knocked out but sat in the armchair now and said she didn't feel too bad herself. But the other thing ...

Her face was red with weeping.

Billy T's bloodstained back-up gun which had caused so much tragedy before he was hit in the arm by a slug from old Herb's Bulldog lay on the floor beside the killer's gun-rig.

Herb had taken the bloodied 'Lightning' Colt and, with it, had shot Billy T's partner, Colehan.

Herb said, 'He's upstairs. I guess he's finished.'

Amos went up the stairs, into the bedroom. Colehan was curled up on the floor just inside the door. He looked strangely misshapen with the bandages across his hairy chest. Also he had both of his hands clasped across his belly. Blood ran through his laced fingers and soaked his long-johns.

His eyes were closed but he was still alive, his breath rasping, then bubbling: horrible sounds.

As Amos bent over him, the man opened agony-filled eyes. He tried to say something, the words croaking, Amos not able to understand them.

Amos said, 'Billy lit out an' left you here to be shot up. Where's Billy going, *amigo?*'

Again the man dying in agony in a welter of blood tried to form words, Amos's face so close to his now that he smelled the breath coming from the tortured lips.

Amos said, 'Tell me. Try. *Try!*'

Nine

Billy T hadn't said much, just mumbled. He was unconscious now. Gracie had bandaged his arm, put it in a sling. It was evident he'd lost an enormous amount of blood, was in a bad way.

Sadie had said she didn't want him there—he was a murderer. Gracie had said they had to do something for him.

Her sister, usually the placid one of the two, was becoming obstreperous, said, 'He's your man. You do something for him if you think you have to.'

Gracie said, 'He's your man as well. You've been with 'im.'

'I never really liked him.'

He needed a doctor. The nearest town was Chicken Creek and there was a doctor there: the twins knew him. But Billy was wanted in Chicken Creek, had killed two men there.

Him and his partner, Colehan, had only been suspects really Gracie said.

'Horseshit,' said Sadie, being vehement.

Yeh, it looked as if Marshal Amos and his two deputies had caught up with the fugitives. Billy was wounded. Maybe Colehan was dead. But where was the law party?

And, if the law party turned up, how would they look upon the two girls taking in the fugitive, succouring him?

But Gracie, at least, had already done that part. And now they were both going through his duds!

He didn't have his gun rig, was unarmed; Gracie had brought it in with her.

It was bloodstained, as was the saddle which the girls hadn't touched. Billy's horse didn't seem to mind the bloodied saddle, however, was browsing quite comfortably outside.

Billy had Bull Durham tobacco and

papers, some coins, including a few silver dollars, a mangy-looking rabbit's foot which was obviously his luck piece (there was no accounting for foibles, Gracie said, rolling the unaccustomed word over on her tongue).

Billy had a couple of greasy playing cards that seemed to have no significance whatsoever, and a small pocket book with numbers on a few of the pages and squiggles that didn't seem to mean anything at all. But Gracie said, 'Maybe he was keeping tally o' something. Money maybe.'

Whether Gracie was right or not, her sister then came up with the clincher, having found it in a sheath sewn on the inside of Billy's pants. She held it up. A roll of greenbacks, tightly wound in black twine, looking enormous in her fist, and she was no midget.

'Will you look at that?' said Sadie.

Billy T was an owlhooter, didn't carry much in the way of identification. But this roll made him look like a rich man indeed.

'Hide it,' exclaimed Gracie. 'For God-sakes, hide it.'

Deke and Lionel had carried the body of old Jube upstairs, placed it on his bed covered by a white sheet.

Herb, although he had managed to put down Colehan, was still in a daze. The gun he had used, the one that had come from Billy T's holster, had been placed on a table; and Herb had placed himself on a chair. He sat staring into space and Deke and Lionel, returning, let him be. Blood had dried upon his face and they figured he'd be all right for a while. Till Amos came down from upstairs anyway.

Mrs Kyle had taken the boy, Benjy, into the kitchen. She had herself fixed a narrow bandage on the shallow groove on her head which just stung now. She was more concerned about the boy, who had quit crying and, though physically unhurt, was behaving like his Dad.

He had been mighty fond of his Grandad. He was in a sort of dream now: maybe that was for the best.

Amos came downstairs and joined the two deputies and Herb in the main room.

He said, 'Colehan was still alive. He's dead. I tried to get him to talk. He tried, but it didn't make much sense ...'

Herb said, 'I never killed a man before.'

'It happens.' Amos went on. 'I had hoped that Colehan might've been able to tell me where Billy might be making for ...'

Herb cut in again, was coming to himself. 'The man's wounded.'

'I know. I can track him I guess. I'll try. We can write Colehan off anyway.'

'They wrote ...' Herb broke off, jerked his head in the direction of upstairs where old Jube lay. Then he hung his head, looked at the floor.

'I know,' said Amos again. 'Colehan didn't have to pay for that. But he did.

And Billy will pay too, I promise you.'

He paused, standing tall in the middle of the floor. The other three men were seated. There were stains on the floor where Jube had fallen, where Billy had fallen.

Amos went on, 'Colehan didn't have much.' The tall man delved round the back of his belt and, when his good right hand appeared again, it held a roll of greenbacks. 'But he had this. Looks like the boys were paid in advance for the job they did, Billy as the shooter, Colehan the back-up. Or maybe they were paid half beforehand, I reckon that'd be more likely. I figured all along that was a hired job on Dealey—and the sheriff just got unlucky is all. I was hoping Colehan would give me something—but he wasn't able to ...'

His voice tailed off. Then broke out again. 'I've got to find Billy.' Suddenly he was like a man talking to himself.

The two boys were in the foothills where they had been chasing a lone maverick who wanted to play games. They figured he was the last of the bunch of strays. The others, contented now, not seeming inclined to roam any more, were grazing on the flatlands. Maybe it was the frisky one who had led them astray in the first place.

He finally got tired of his games and they were able to loop him and take him down to the rest and drive them back to the ranch, leaving them just in sight of the outbuildings.

It was quiet over there.

They were surprised to see a figure appear and start waving to them. A figure that they didn't at first recognize, though not a menacing one in any way at all, the waving hands empty.

The Mexican boy said, 'Eet ees Deke from town. He helped us weeth some horses once, remember?'

'I remember,' said the half-Apache boy. They moved on into shock and tragedy.

And, finally, it had to be left to them as

they followed orders given to them by the steely-eyed moustached marshal they had heard called Amos.

The family knew that old Jube would want his resting place to be near the ranch where he'd spent his last, happy years.

The law party, knowing the family would understand, that old Jube certainly would understand, went on their quest again.

They knew the direction Billy T had taken. There was blood. There was scuffed earth. And young Benjy had seen the wounded man ride out.

Amos, walking at first, leading his horse, said that it almost looked as if the man was backtracking. Or maybe his horse had been taking him, willy-nilly.

Amos sent Lionel, if reluctantly, off to town to get the doctor and the preacher: both would be needed.

The trail Billy T had struck certainly wasn't the one back to town. Even if Billy meandered and his path crossed with that of the pudgy young deputy, with Billy wounded an' all, Amos figured that the deputy could handle him. Lionel was going up in Amos's estimation all the time, though he couldn't quite figure why this was: he was just working on his instincts.

Back at the ranch the two hands would bury Colehan, clear up after him. It would be as if that particular owlhooter had never existed. The house would be put right, Mrs Kyle and the boy Benjy would see to that.

The man, Herb, had wanted to ride with the law party, but Amos had vetoed this and Herb's missus had backed that. Herb was not what you might call outa the woods yet. The sooner the doc from town saw him, the better. And the preacher could do the last honours for old Jube

Although Billy T wouldn't have been expected to take the trail he had, would've been expected in fact to go in the opposite direction, the law pair who now remained on the trail had to take in account that the man was wounded. Bleeding badly too: they'd seen signs of that.

After a bit Deke said, 'You know where this trail's leadin' us if we go straight as an arrow, don't you, Amos?'

'Yes,' said the marshal. 'The Caracterus twins' place.'

Ten

'If we want to keep this money we have to finish 'im off,' said Gracie.

Sadie gave a little gasp. 'We can't do that. I've never done ...'

'Hell,' cut in her sister, 'you've done everything else. You got a better idea?'

Billy T was coming to his senses when he heard the words. He opened his eyes to slits. He could see the two girls, though not too clearly. Right now he certainly couldn't tell 'em apart. He figured that the one nearest to him, bending forward a little, was Gracie. He had recently shared a bed with that cold-blooded snake-bitch. She hadn't been cold-blooded then.

She'd meant every word of what she'd just said, Billy was as sure of that as he was of the other thing: they had his money!

Gracie was the toughest one of the two—and they were both greedy bitches, so Sadie would come round to her twin's way of thinking.

Sadie, quiet now as if cogitating.

Billy's wounded arm felt as if it was tearing itself away from his shoulder, and the rest of his upper body was on fire.

He felt that Gracie was bending closer to him. Then he saw her clearer—as if she were *looming*. Did she have a knife?

He couldn't see a knife.

Slit-eyed, he saw her hands. They seemed huge. Then they were out of sight.

The pillow was removed with surprising gentleness from beneath his head. He knew then what was about to happen next.

Gracie was acting; and there were no more words from her sister now. In fact, Sadie was momentarily out of sight of the man on the bed. The man who had seemed half-dead already—but was suddenly imbued with desperate life.

Wounded arm limp, swathed. But the other arm shooting upwards, a balled fist at the end of it. The fist smashing like a cannonball into Gracie's pretty, but now suddenly contorted features.

She screamed and staggered backwards, the pillow falling from her hands to the bed. Billy leapt upwards and out of the bed like a maniac. His stockinged feet hit the floor. His shirt and boots had been taken from him but otherwise he was fully dressed.

Gracie had her hands to her face. Blood came through her fingers. Sadie was a distance away and seemed to be cowering, her eyes staring, her mouth working wordlessly.

Billy went between them and hit the door which was open to let in the breeze. Sheer fury carried him on. He only had one arm. His torso burned. He had to find a weapon.

He stumbled, almost fell. Rising, he saw his horse, head turned towards its master.

The man stumbled forward, lurching, wavering. But he reached his goal. He yanked the rifle—those bitches had missed that!—from its saddle-boot. He turned, cradling the long gun, resting the butt awkwardly on his side as he leaned against the horse's flank.

In front of him the door was flung wide open with a crash and Gracie came through. She had gotten a knife from some place, big, wicked-looking, almost a cleaver, Her bloodstained face looked demoniacal. Her eyes glared as she came at him.

Billy pressed the trigger of the rifle twice. It bucked; it hurt him. Only the horse held him up.

Gracie seemed to be stopped in her tracks as if she'd run at breakneck speed into a wall.

She seemed to bounce. And then she went flat, her legs kicking up in the air, flouncing her skirts, revealing her voluminous, lace-edged drawers.

She lay flat, stretched, the knife a few inches away from her clawing fingers and the dust settling around her. It was as if Billy's eyes suddenly had second sight, and it was brilliant. He saw everything gleefully. He heard things too. He heard Sadie wail like a sorrowful coyote. But she did not appear.

The weakness came upon him again. The house shimmered before him, and the body on the ground was like a doll. He knew that if he went in after Sadie, she would have the drop on him, would have time if he even happened to reach the door.

He wanted the money. So badly he wanted the money that he had earned, that had brought him to this!

But if he was going to save his own life—and that was on the turn of the cards now—he had to get away. Maybe he'd get help ...

He managed to climb on to the horse ... and the horse took him around the side of the building. Here there was a narrow window which looked out on to the chicken run, the fowl squawking as the snorting beast galloped by.

The window smashed, drawing Billy's attention—it was all like a dream. But then awareness went through him like a sudden arrow as he saw the snout of a rifle poke through the shattered glass and remembered how good a rifle-shot Sadie was. He had expected her to run out to her sister. But Gracie was dead—and Sadie had acted fast.

He hardly heard the shot.

He felt something kick him in the side, high up. He was knocked sideways in the saddle and only instinct held him on, one hand gripping the reins.

Then he was engulfed by pain as if by boiling acid—and it was worse than it had ever been before.

But the horse carried him on.

He didn't know how long he was carried before he fell off; and the horse, like a wild thing, galloped on without him.

He knew he was dying, his blood running from him and pooling in the sparse grass and the soil beneath it. He could not see very well.

They had his money, had hidden it. He had nothing and soon he would be *nothing*. No, one of the twins was dead. Gracie, his favourite: that was a laughable thing.

Would the other one come after him, make sure? He would like to shoot her too, but he had dropped his rifle back at the place and had no other weapon.

He tried to look back but could only see a shimmering haze and if anything moved they were ghosts. He didn't think anything moved.

The pain was less. He was able to turn slowly as he lay. He couldn't see the horse. The wild bastard!

That one had always been a wild bastard!

Something dug into Billy T's side. He groped, and he found the long stick. Some animal had been chewing it, peeling it with sharp teeth. One end was sharp-pointed. Billy took it up.

As he scratched the name in the dust, he began to laugh, feeling the sound in his head like the rattle of pebbles in a tin can.

He was still laughing as he died.

When Deke and Amos reached the little spread Sadie was standing over her sister's body pointing a rifle at them. When, through her bleary, tear-filled eyes, she saw them clearly she lowered the weapon.

The two men carried the body into the house and laid it down in Gracie's own bed.

Sadie told them what had happened.

'I got 'im,' she said. 'But he didn't fall out of the saddle.'

'Where's the money, girl?' Amos asked.

'What money? I don't ...'

The man cut in, his voice sharpening, his cold, bluey-grey eyes boring into hen 'Don't try and snow me, I ain't got the time. You must have found the money. It's blood money. Give it back. Otherwise we'll have to search the place. 'Less you'd like to try and shoot us of course.'

The girl rose. The man said, more gently, 'I'll see you get some kind of reward and your sister buried decently.'

'Best thing, honey,' said Deke.

She brought the wad of notes to them. Amos counted, said, 'Billy T got the lion's share it seems. He was the shooter all right.'

He turned to Deke, looked at him levelly, went on, 'There's a small wagon here, I saw it. I want you to take Sadie an' her sister to town.'

'I don't think ...'

'You're my deputy.' The older man's voice had steel in it again. 'If you want to stay that way you do as I bid.'

'All right, Amos.'

It didn't take Amos long to find the body of Billy T.

He saw the strange squiggles in the dust and, out of the saddle, got down on one knee to examine the marks.

A name written with a bloodstained stick.

Messages from the dead.

But, at least, Sheriff Beaky Teal had been able to speak before he passed on. One word before death took him. Rowel. And here in the bloodsoaked dust lay the young man, spurless now, that the rowel had belonged to, that with its fellow he had once worn with pride.

In the dust, the word *Swithin*. What did it mean? It looked like a name. Was it a name?

Amos had all the money now, and the two men who'd earned it, by conspiring to perform an execution, lay dead.

One would be buried soon. And Amos figured that, being the law, he had to take the carcass of the other one back to Chicken Creek.

He saw the horse in the distance and

he put his fingers to his lips and emitted a shrill whistle. The beast came tentatively forward. He was lathered, his eyes somewhat askance. He looked as if he'd galloped off wildly, maybe for quite a spell, had come back through sheer bloody curiosity.

He sniffed at the body, then looked at the live man enquiringly.

'He's still gonna ride you,' Amos said. 'Stand still.'

The horse was tractable, allowed himself to be loaded with the corpse, his eyes rolling at the new man doing this new thing. An intelligent, feisty beast.

When Amos got back to Chicken Creek he discovered he was in time for the funeral of Sheriff Teal and Dealey the Dealer. He hadn't expected to be back so soon.

Eleven

Deke had arrived in town with Sadie, and her sister's body. A third funeral was quickly arranged.

The town's star preacher had gone with the doc to Herb Kyle's little spread where folks had been hurt and one, old Jube, had died. Jube had been a popular old cuss. Some of the townsfolk wanted to go to his funeral, the burying out on the land on which Jube had spent his declining happy years. Some folks did leave. Others decided they'd go later to pay their respects.

Some folks just didn't know what to do, what to think even. These were bad times. Come so suddenly, too.

Chicken Creek was in a state of mourning, even after many of them had seen the bloody corpse of Billy T and learned that Billy's sidekick, Colehan was probably already under the sod, deader than worn-out, thrown-away boots. The way Billy would go also: no high Boot Hill for him.

With the absence of the preacher, soon officiating miles away out on the prairie, his place was taken by his cousin and helper, a small but handsome young man with a surprisingly sonorous voice, who was lately favoured by many of the congregation, particularly the younger womenfolk.

After dumping Billy T's body at the undertaking parlour and, before doing much else, Marshal Amos went to the bank and had the boodle he'd collected put in the strongroom for safe-keeping.

He then joined Stella and Molly, with whom he would attend the buryings on the hill outside the town. They were, of course, mighty glad to see him back so soon, for whatever reason.

The local undertaker had worked very hard. Soon all that was left in his parlour was the lonely cadaver of Billy T, who would be buried later. Everybody who had wanted to take a look at the killer's corpse had already done so and were now wending their way to more solemn occasions.

Boot Hill was thronged with people. It seemed that all of the town was there. The kids had a day off from school and were for a while all on their best behaviour—until the whole thing was finished that is, and then, in common with many of the young cowboys who'd taken time off for the buryings, were ready now to dispel their sorrows, their waitings.

Some of the cowboys had known the twin called Gracie. After seeing her sister in the last resting place, the other twin Sadie had been transported back to her home by two willing volunteers, for Deputy Deke, who'd brought her here, had business with Deputy Lionel and the new town marshal.

Kids ran pell-mell down the hill around the law trio. Amos had already left Stella and Molly who were making their way home. Amos and his two sidekicks repaired to the jail which was empty now. They sat down in the office as if for a council of war.

'What did you find at the twins' place, Deke?' Amos wanted to know.

Deke gave him the book that had belonged to Billy T. Lionel already knew about this. A small tattered notebook with dog-eared grimy leaves and peeling cardboard covers, the yellowing pages with marks that, at first, seemed to mean nothing. Like a tally book, Amos said, though, and the others agreed with him.

Then Amos said, stabbing a finger at the yellowing, dog-eared pages. 'These numbers, they've got no signs ahead of 'em, but they could be money. The prices Billy earned for his particler line o' work, and we know what that was. Some of them have letters after 'em. Two letters mostly, which could be the initials of the folks who paid.'

He began to delve through the notebook, which was indeed very much like a rancher's tally book, going towards the back pages. Although he hadn't bothered to divulge the knowledge to his two sidekicks, he had counted the amount of money comprising the rolls that had come from the pockets of Billy and his partner Colehan.

He hadn't counted any odd *dinero* that the two had had on them, although he'd stashed that in the local bank also.

He found the amount listed at the end of the book and a plus mark against it which seemed to indicate that the amount had only been a down payment, with more to come when the job was completed.

Billy had definitely been the leader of the two men, the professional assassin. He had split the money and given Colehan the smaller amount.

The plus mark was followed by two letters. A.S. Suddenly it was as if Amos's two companions weren't with him any more. He was thinking deeply.

He remembered the word that the dying Billy had scratched in the dirt with a pointed branch. It had read like 'Swithin'. It had certainly begun with a crooked S. Was that word, name, the surname of the person who'd hired the two killers or, at least, had spoken to Billy and paid him the first slice of *dinero?*

Amos was used to playing his cards close to his chest, used to watching the dealer, the dealer's eyes, the eyes of the other players as they took their cards, glanced at them as if with disinterest as a good gambler would. But now Amos was the dealer as well as the player and he took a chance and wished for a flush hand.

He said, 'Have either of you two young gentlemen heard of somebody called Swithin?'

Deke looked at Lionel, said, 'You hear what he called us, pardner?'

The pudgy deputy's smooth face broke into a smile which didn't quite reach his eyes. He said, 'I heard. I reckon he's got good taste.'

He paused; both men were looking at him then. He went on, 'There was a gamblin' town in Arizona run by somebody of that name. Swithin.' He looked at Deke. 'I think you an' me talked of it once, mentioned that we'd both been through there. If it's still going, hell, it's quite a place, ain't it?'

'Yeh.' Deke seemed to be cogitating, his handsome face set, his eyes hooded. Then he said briskly, looking at nobody in particular, 'In some rocky land not far from the border. Used to be an Injun settlement or somep'n. Them very old Injun tribes that used to be there back in history. First off it was called Terida, somp'n like that. Most folks now just call it Gamblers' Town. Yeh, I guess it's still runnin'. It was run by a gent called Hiram Swithin partnered by an old Mexican called Don Hernandero, somep'n like that.'

'Wild,' said Amos softly. 'Maybe just a sort of coincidence. I personally never heard of Gamblers' Town in Arizona. Still an' all, maybe I've been out of touch with things like that in recent times, not travellin' like I used to. I wonder if Dealey the Dealer ever happened along there.'

'Could well have done I guess,' said Lionel. 'A jasper like him who always seemed to have a deck of cards in his hand.'

Deke, wordless, was nodding his dark head slowly up and down.

Not long after, Amos went back to The Armoury.

He looked around the shadowed place with the things softly gleaming. So many weapons here. But weapons didn't always have to be used for war or for fighting. He had some of the best hunting rifles ever made, firing shot that could bring down a bird or an animal with but little damage to the carcass so that a huntsman's hound could pick it up gently in its jaws.

But there were other things. Killing weapons. And sometimes they just had to be used too. There was two-legged scum walking in the West who were worse than any animals. Animals seldom killed their own in the ways that humans did.

He went through to the back. Molly was out with some playmates from school. Stella was on her own.

'I have to go riding again, honey,' he said. 'I don't know how long I'll be gone.'

He had had peace in the shop, she knew that. She loved him and she had peace with him. She knew he had felt some of this himself (he was a quiet man anyway): she knew he would never do anything to hurt her and Molly. But she had sensed the old restlessness coming on him.

And now he wore a badge again. It had not at first been of his own choosing, she knew that. But he was perhaps the only one who could really take Sheriff Teal's place, and the genial lawman called Beaky had been his friend.

And another man had been murdered literally before Amos's eyes.

'I will get some provisions ready for you, sweetheart,' she said.

His two deputies had wanted to come with him but he had said they must watch the town. They couldn't argue with him. He was a loner again. He was doing what he could do best. He was Marshal Amos again as he had been in other times, in other places: there was no one else like him.

He knew that Lionel and Deke firmly believed that one of them should go with him, back him up if needs be. But which one? He didn't in his mind sell either one of them short. Neither of them had been able to tell him much about his destination—or maybe they hadn't wanted to. They were both, in their separate ways, reticent young men. But many Westerners were like that. Amos was himself by way of being like that.

Thinking like a loner, talking like a loner, operating like a loner.

The deputies' instructions about the marshal's route to take had been sketchy. Their knowledge of Terida, Gamblers' Town, had been sketchy, from the old days. Did such young men have what is called a past, he'd wondered? Was this why he'd decided to go alone on his quest, leaving them to look after their town?

Yeh, it was his town also now you might say. But had any town he had known—and he had known so many!—really been *his?* Maybe this quest, if it proved to be his last one, would give him the answer to that question.

Maybe Gamblers' Town didn't even have any being any more, was a ghost town. Maybe it had become just an ordinary sort of community. If so where was the man whose name was Swithin—and his partner, Don Hernandero?

Amos rode. He meant to ride all the way. No railroad, no stage. He would rest, take sustenance, ask guarded questions. That was the way he usually operated. A loner on a horse, the piebald stallion he had bought when he first hit Chicken Creek. A tough, affable beast called Rags because his tail looked that way, after he'd almost had it chewed to the stub by a wickedly fractious mule, dead now after being kicked in the head by a furious screaming cayuse. But the tail had never grown back properly and sometimes wagged like a puppy's.

Amos began to hear about the town, the town called Terida: Gamblers' Town.

Twelve

It lay in a valley with the craggy, low-lying but treacherous hills on one side and the equally treacherous badlands on the other, There was lush ground each side of it but not much of that. A creek watered the town. There were a few smallholdings but nothing that could be called a ranch.

Horses were sold but very little other livestock. A man on the run on a worn-out steed could get another cayuse but had to pay dearly for it. The horse corrals were a sideline of Don Hernandero's, and he gave no man anything. Men escaping across the desert to evade the law didn't always make it to the other side, but their new horses sometimes did and were returned to their post to await another sucker.

The best and by far the quickest way to

approach the town was through the pass in the hills, craggy, dangerous, to be carefully negotiated. But folks with gambling fever did this very frequently, for to reach their destination through the easier trails which circumvented the perilous crags would take them an extra two days. Wagons came that way, and the caravans with the girls, and the fit-up stagers and medicine men.

Policed by hard men with ready guns, Terida was open to all, the fleecers and those to be fleeced, though even the former were usually skimmed nearly to the bone by the minions of Don Hernandero and his partner, Hiram Swithin, the elderly lords of all they surveyed.

Amos and his horse, Rags, were well-rested, having stopped over a while in a blustering town which somebody had dubbed Tombstone. Silver had been found in the hills near there and, if the vein didn't run out, Tombstone was likely to become greatly famous.

The man wasn't wearing his badge and,

unless watchers took a good look at his armoury, he could be taken for just another drifter with a poke he was likely to lose in Gamblers' Town. There were watchers. There always were, some place around.

There were some in the rocks now and they greeted the new pilgrim—riding alone there on the rocky terrain—with but scant courtesy. They remained incognito as they used their long guns.

Amos was always wary. It had been part of his make-up for more years than he could count.

But he hadn't expected this.

However, the first rifleman was too eager—or maybe he just wasn't good enough.

The slug went over Amos's head, didn't even take his hat off. He dropped from the saddle, away from the direction of the shot; and the echo was a ghostly thing. He slapped his horse's flank.

The stallion galloped ahead, hooves clattering, dust and shale spitting, hissing.

There was a sudden barrage, a cluster of shots, the echoes rolling. Amos wasn't using his horse as a shield: that was something he couldn't do. The beast was out of harm's way. The man, moving like an eel, had found sparse cover behind a small outcrop of rocks and crouched down, bellied the earth.

He had his long-barrelled Dragoon in one hand and, in the other, his new back-up weapon taken from the pouch in back of his belt, a smaller double-action pistol of English make, ideal for thumb-action on the hammer, fast.

Maybe the bushwhackers—he figured now there were two of 'em—should have used hand-guns. The range wasn't long. Maybe they hadn't planned enough, or had taken a sudden opportunity to rob a lone stranger on the trail.

The heavy modified Dragoon boomed and the recoil tingled his shoulder, a satisfying thing that he had long enjoyed. Two shots, rolling together as one as the echoes took them. He laid the big gun in the dust and fanned the hammer of the smaller one, sending a hail of lead up at the rocks. He had that pair pinpointed already. But he couldn't aim straight with his head in the dust, had to show himself a mite.

Something that felt like a red-hot branding iron seared his left arm, causing him to drop the English pistol. Almost as a reflex action, though, he worked the Dragoon and, peering through the black smoke as the echoes rang in his ears and ricochets screamed, he saw the man tumble from the rocks and roll and become still, in a crumpled heap.

There was the pattering of dust, infinitesimal, all that was left until there was the clatter of hooves on rocks, that noise coming from the rocks above the man, motionless, whom Amos had brought down.

He whistled his horse. The piebald stallion came around the bend of the trail and Amos leapt into the saddle, stashing the two pistols, taking the rifle from its scabbard.

He hit the trail, reached a gap which had probably let the two bushwhackers in, immediately saw the flying horseback-man, a riderless mount keeping pace.

Amos raised his rifle. Then he realized the range was too long and he lowered the weapon, peered out at the dustcloud till it disappeared, the two horses, the man. And only the dying sun was left.

Maybe the two bushwhackers had left it too late at that.

Amos turned the stallion about. He dismounted, went to the body in the rocks.

The youngish, stubble-chinned man lay in a twisted position, but his head was caught in a small declivity, and the staring eyes looked up at the dying red sun.

Like an inquisitive turkey this jasper had popped his head up too soon and Amos, the old turkey-shooter, had got him plumb centre and he had a third eye in the middle of his forehead.

Amos wondered whether this one had been the marksman who hadn't been as good as he might. His rifle, a Winchester repeater that looked as good as new, lay near the corpse's twisted arm. He wouldn't get any practise with that long gun any more and that was a fact.

Amos got down on one knee and searched the body while the piebald stallion called Rags watched him curiously from below.

Amos took the man's hand-gun, a serviceable Peacemaker, and tucked it in his belt. A knife too, and some chawing baccy, a stub of pencil but no notebook or bill or paper of any kind. A small roll of notes and a few coins, a crumpled red ribbon that had probably come from some whore's hair. This one didn't look like a married, settling-down sort of cuss.

Nothing else. An owlhooter, thought

Amos, a man who didn't like to be identified.

He picked up the Winchester, much like his own long gun, but newer. Maybe new to the man, likely—had he needed more practice?

Amos could tote the extra rifle and the other two smaller weapons, the Colt, the well-used claspknife. He wished he had the spare horse. But that cayuse would be long gone now, together with the second bushwhacker and his mount. Were they making for Terida?

He put the body over the front of his saddle. The stallion called Rags snorted scornfully but did not balk.

They went more slowly than they'd done before and they came out of the end of the pass.

The red sun was almost gone but still bathed in its light the valley below and the cluster of buildings which made up Gamblers' Town. Tight, clustered, as if waiting, the dusky red rays bathing the roofs. A town yet not a town. One main street and the buildings clustered neatly around it.

People moving about. A cart or two. A line of horses at a hitching rack. Business already. But maybe this place never completely stopped, never completely slept.

Folks stopping to stare now at the horseman with a body over the front of his saddle.

'Who's that?' one old-timer was heard to say. But did he mean the sacklike body, or did he mean the horseman who sat upright, arrogantly, in the saddle?

One other wizened oldster was more forthright than others and, whether by accident or design, blocked the horseman's passage and he drew his mount to a halt while the dying sun threw long shadows on the hard-baked street.

Greatly daring, the old man bent in a rheumatic way and peered at the face of the corpse which was slung so inelegantly across the front of the saddle.

The rider said, 'He tried to bushwhack me on the trail. Do you know him?'

'Name's Ben something-or-other. That's all I know.'

'Who's he work for?'

'Nobody in partic'ler. Picks up what he can I reckon.' The oldster looked up at Amos.

'He had a pardner. Did you see somebody ride into town fast ahead o' me?'

'Cain't say I did, mister.'

'Where's the law in this town?'

'I guess you cain't exactly call this a town, mister. And we ain't got anything you can partic'larly call law either.'

'Where's the undertaker's place then?'

The old man turned and pointed. 'Right ahead. Red sign swingin' in the breeze. Our buryin' man is a sort of humourist.'

'I see. I'm glad you told me that. I might've taken that place for the local bordello.'

'That's back on the edge o' town. You passed it comin' in. Big place. Very respectable-lookin'. Where the girls soften up the suckers before lettin' 'em down this way.' The old man stepped backwards and the piebald stallion and his rider and their burden went sedately past him.

The shadows were longer. The people stood. Not a lot of them. Staring. Somebody asked the question again and a name was spoken softly. A man like that might be known in a place like this.

Thirteen

The Terida undertaker was a plump, jolly man with the mannerisms of a drummer selling ladies' doo-dads. He greeted Amos as if he were a long-lost friend—and bearing gifts to boot. He looked at the corpse of Ben with a professional's eye, albeit with a sort of twinkle. Ben gazed up at him owlishly with his own three eyes, reclining as he was comfortably now on a well-scrubbed trestle table.

Amos gave the buryin' man the same short speil he had given the oldster out on the street.

'Fine shooting,' said the plump, beaming man. 'An' I guess it had to happen to Ben sooner or later.'

He was more forthcoming than the oldster in the street had been, going on

129

to tell his visitor that Ben's bosom pard went by the name of Greeley and he had ridden past in the street not long before Amos turned up.

'Like his ass was on fire,' chuckled the buryin' man.

But he didn't know where Greeley might have gone or where he usually hung out, said, 'Skulked in holes like rats, him and Ben.'

The saloon, thought Amos, everybody turned up at a local saloon sooner or later. He had been right in front of it when the old-timer had confronted him. It had a façade nobody but a short-sighted idiot was likely to miss, calling itself The Ideale House, with an E at the end.

He left Rags the stallion at the livery stable. Nobody was asking him questions and, if folks still looked at him, it was in a surreptitious way.

The Ideale House was a building with a newly painted burgundy and black frontage, long, imposing, though already blistering here and there where the sun struck it most. Looking up, Amos figured the structure to be of two storeys. But it had a towering false front that made it look a floor taller than that.

The batwings, as he breasted them, were wider than usual and didn't wobble or creak; and the sight that met his gaze then, now all the lights were on and there was twilight outside, made his dust-filled eyes widen. His throat was dusty also, and parched. Looking about him, he wended his way to the bar.

It was early yet but the place was comfortably full with space to move around. Nobody paid the newcomer much mind as he took whiskey and turned about, elbow on bar-top, heel hooked on brass rail near a brass spittoon that shone like gold.

There was a gambling area and a dance area and a stage with burgundy curtains drawn across it and a tall piano already being played by a small man perched on a stool and a pile of magazines, obligatory striped black and white vest and twinkling fingers, bordello-type music but none the worse for that.

There was nobody too near Amos, but the barkeep still hovered and, turning to him, the lean moustached stranger asked, 'You know Greeley, pardner? I'm lookin' for Greeley.'

'I guess he'll be in later,' the man said. 'You a friend of his?'

'Sort of.'

Maybe this stranger was the law. The 'keep didn't ask.

Amos wasn't wearing his new badge, had more sense than to stick his nose way out like that, was more out of his jurisdiction now than a bishop in a brothel.

The barkeep was a helpful cuss, saying about a half-hour later, 'Here's Greeley, suh.' And Greeley was way this side of the batwings when Amos turned towards him.

Greeley had made a bad move, shouldn't have been here at all tonight, maybe was too stupid to realize that. He was even more stupid when he let his shock, his recognition of the man he and his partner had tried to bushwhack, show in his face, the dropped lower lip, the startled eyes.

He turned and went back through the batwings, leaving them swinging wildly after him. Amos followed, butting past people, then swinging lower. He went through one of the wide batwings at the edge, crablike, turning abruptly left, his gun already in his hand, hardly aware that he'd drawn it, but lifting it now. But Greeley wasn't shooting, he was running, the thud of his heels resounding, then the noise dying.

An alley ran alongside the big establishment, a ghostly echo, Amos following that echo.

Keeping closely to the wall, moving catlike, on his toes, still half-crouching. No light at all here, the darkness deepening all the time until the corner, the breeze, the openness.

A row of privies. And a gun blasting from behind them. Wood-chips hitting Amos's face, making him flinch. Crouching, he moved from one corner to the other, aiming to confuse the shooter who, he figured, couldn't be anybody else but Greeley, a burly, lolloping cuss with a face like a horse.

The shooting stopped. Amos hadn't triggered even once. And maybe Greeley was running again. Amos taking a chance, moving along the back of the buildings, staring at the row of privies, four in all. He'd seen plenty worse. In the half-light the narrow edifices looked like a row of soldiers at attention.

Just in time, Amos ducked behind a pile of rubbish. Things weren't really as salubrious out here as they were out front in this neat Gamblers' Town which, as one old-timer had said, was hardly a real township at all. *Just in time,* a slug buzzing over Amos's head, where his head had been a split moment before.

He heard the slug thunk into the wooden wall behind him. And the sound must've covered that other one, instinct only causing Amos to turn. He saw the swinging weapon, looked like a shotgun, only a vague figure behind it; then something that felt like the hoof of a wild and frantic horse struck his temple and exploded his brain in blackness.

The blackness was still there when he opened his eyes. But, turning his head slowly, he saw a thin line of light from a grating in a wall. He was in a cellar and there was the smell of apples.

His hands were lashed behind him and his legs were trussed together at the ankles. His head felt as if it were full of bees, but he wasn't hurting any place else as far as he could make out with the limited movements available to him.

He lowered his head gently to the floor which seemed to be made of hard-baked earth, hard but not too unpleasant. Still and all, he'd never much liked the smell of apples.

Stella was awakened by the sound of young Molly moaning in the room next door. It became obvious to Stella that her daughter's bad tooth was bedeviling her once more. Stella had been restless herself, missing Amos in the bed beside her, worrying about him. She had gotten used to being a storekeeper's wife with a settled home, even an occupation, the respect of a community, new and valued friends, a husband who was with her much of the time, not off riding in perilous ways as he used to be.

But this had all changed again as she had feared it might, and Amos wasn't getting any younger and she feared for him greatly.

Stella had put pepper on Molly's bad tooth and, more recently, bathed the gums in oil of cloves, which had seemed to work better than anything else. Molly, who like many people, young or old, was a mite scared of dentristry, hadn't wanted any part of it if such could be avoided. Stella, too, had wanted to save the tooth, but now, with the pale early morning light coming through the window and the sounds of the youngster suffering in the room next door, she knew that something must be done *muy pronto,* as Amos might have said.

She knew that the local medico, who also doubled as a dentist (a pretty good one) was famous for early rising, as well as being an avid fisherman, out catching scaly titbits before his patients appeared at his door.

Maybe the fish aren't biting very well right now, Stella thought. In any case she might catch the old boy before he went on a morning pasear. If she pulled up her socks, that is, which she commenced to do in double-quick time, calling, 'I'm coming, honey.'

Molly was already out of bed, pacing

around the room in her robe and filling the air with her own particular brand of swearing, nothing obscene or profane, but words like 'tarnation', 'pesky', 'gosh' and 'goldarn', 'dadblast' and *'outdacious'* plus a few more jaw-twisters she'd made up by her ownself.

Protesting, but now only half-heartedly, she was made respectable and marched out on to the morning street.

They saw the doc right off. He was talking to the elderly bank guard, a retired lawman who hadn't, however, hung up his shooters, who always went to an early-opening cantina for coffee before repairing to the bank where the banker himself, accompanied by both a male and female teller, unlocked the doors for him.

Hearing footsteps, both oldsters turned and greeted Stella and Molly with bright 'good mornings'.

The sun wasn't up and there was a morning haze which interfered with visibility. There didn't seem yet to be anybody else on the street except the two elderly gentlemen and the two female persons.

The older female person opened her mouth to return the morning's greetings—the younger one had her lips tightly closed—and it stayed open, no words issuing, as a tremendous explosion resounded in the ears of the quartet and shook the ground beneath their feet.

Their ears rang. Their eyes stared. Stella saw the bank guard's mouth form words, appropriate ones: 'The bank!' And the doc was staring past Stella and Molly also and, like automats powered by machinery, they turned about. They were still staring as the bank guard and the doc ran past them, the plumper, slow-moving medico in the rear.

Black smoke was pouring from the bank. Through the drifting veil of this a figure could be seen running towards it with three horses on a string. Then two other men ran out of the bank doors with sacks in their hands, guns, their heads turning towards the irritating early-morning townsmen running towards them.

Maybe they hadn't expected that. But there were only two elderly townies anyway.

But the one in front had a gun out. And he started shooting.

The echoes were dying. Half-turning, the doc shouted, 'Take cover, you two. Move!'

They didn't need any second telling, scuttled for the sidewalk, Stella almost dragging her daughter.

They crouched behind a convenient horse trough.

One of the bank robbers had gone down, a bullet in him from the bank guard's gun. He had dropped the boodle he carried. His partner bent and picked it up, thus escaping the elderly guard's second shot which only took his hat off.

'Go get 'em, Mr Trumble,' yelled young Molly who seemed to have entirely forgotten her toothache.

'Keep your head down,' her mother admonished her.

The doc, who never carried anything more lethal than a scalpel, had taken meagre cover on the sidewalk ahead of the two females.

The younker with the three horses had produced a gun now and was doing some trigger-snapping. He wasn't too accurate, though, having to hold the cayuses at the same time: the gunfire was making them restive and they wanted to be away from it.

The second man snapped a couple of shots at bank guard Trumble who gasped, hit, dropped on one knee.

The younker with the horses stopped shooting, scared of hitting his pard who was running for the horses now, leaving his bank partner in a still heap on the ground behind him. Swinging the two sacks in one hand and his gun in the other, the running man wasn't doing any shooting now. His pard, upright, holstered his gun and used both hands to hold the fractious horses.

There was the sudden clatter of hooves, but the sound didn't come from the beasts in charge of the third bank robber. These hooves had a rhythm; they galloped; and the horseman came down the street from the direction which lay behind the two females crouching behind the horse trough and the rotund doctor against a wall.

The horseman wheeled his horse around the stooping figure of Mr Trumble. He yelled something. He had a gun in his hand and he opened up.

Two startled faces were turned towards him and, behind the owners of those faces, the three getaway steeds began to jitter. One even began to violently perform, succeeded eventually in snatching his reins from the holder's hands and started to do a buck and wing on the main street of Chicken Creek.

The young man was off-balance, still trying to hold the other two mounts.

The man wasn't really a man—now he was just a wide-eyed scared-looking kid.

He let two of the horses go, vaulted into the saddle of the other one, drove it into a wild gallop. The other two horses followed. The speeding cortège, swathed in dust, were soon beyond the reach of even the longest reaching barrel and bullet of any gun.

The remaining bank robber was alone in the middle of the street, his bags at his feet and his hands full of two guns bucking, flaming, thundering. He was already hit, though, and his own shots were high as the strange horseman rode down on him, shooting, finally driving him down flat and still.

Then there was only the drifting gun-smoke covering the morning haze as the sun began to peep out of a cloudless sky and the echoes waned and then died while a small breeze drove the acrid smell of cordite away.

The strange horseman seemed to be

mainly clad in black. His horse was a dun-coloured stallion. The man bent from the saddle and inspected the two bodies. He leaned further from the saddle and picked up the two sacks that had been dropped in the dust.

Bank guard Trumble was on his feet and limping forward. Stella was trying to shield her daughter's eyes from the two bodies. 'I know that man,' Stella said to nobody in particular.

Coming to full standing, mother and daughter moved forward to join the doctor.

All three of them heard Trumble say in answer to the young rider's question, 'I'm all right, thanks. Just a burn on my knee. Put me down momentarily.'

The young rider holstered his gun, made a gesture, said, 'Those two are goners, the other was just a kid for the horses I guess, an' we won't see 'im again.'

'That was some shootin',' said Trumble.

'Well, I guess I had the drop.'

By this time the horseman was facing

the four people who looked up at him.

Stella said, 'Hello, Parley.'

The young horseman said, 'Hello, Stella. Molly.'

Molly said, 'Hello, Mr Masters.'

'I didn't know it was you two at first,' said Parley Masters. 'Where's Amos? I expected to see him.'

Stella said, 'He isn't here right now. But you turned up when you were needed, didn't you?'

'He surely did,' said Mr Trumble.

More folks were appearing on the street. Lawmen Deke and Lionel came in sight. Parley saw them before the other three folk did because he was facing that way. He leaned forward in his saddle, squinted, stared. Then he said: 'Hello there, Deke.'

They were all turning as Deke came to a dead stop, staring, his mouth half-open. Then he said, 'Hello, Parley.'

PART 2

Hangman's Bait

Fourteen

Gamblers' Town, also known as Terida had, years gone by, been an Apache settlement, Chihuahua or Mescalero, maybe a mixture of both: they didn't always fight among themselves. Sometimes they banded together to go up against their traditional enemies, the Comanches or against the polyglot, renegade *comancheros* who preyed on anybody for gain, took Indian scalps for bounty. But as white settlers moved down to the borderlands—and after the Civil War they came in droves—and were backed by their blue-coat soldier-boys, the Apaches, and all the border Indians, had a common foe.

Mexican troops harried them also, while they took their revenge on innocent white folk, the settlers and their wives and children, the cattle and sheep herders, the carpet-baggers, the stage coaches and covered wagons and soon, the puffing, screeching 'iron horses'.

The people of the settlement of Terida—though they probably called it something else in the Indian way—were driven into the border hills by *Norte-Americano* troops and descended from time to time to pillage and rape and murder all the people that were not their *people,* the chosen ones whose land this was.

A Mexican sheep-man called Manuel Hernandero saw a prime opportunity and moved his stock, his herders and his women into the valley which they began to call Terida. There was water there and shelter. The Apaches, always on the roam as was their nature, always attacking and retreating in their cunning guerilla way, hadn't done much with the camp, had only left odorous reminders of their sojourn there. The peon women were set to their clean-up task and the men ran the sheep.

This was not prime cattle country. But sheep weren't so particular: they chewed everything to the bone anyway. Manuel Hernandero had buyers on both sides of the border. He began to prosper. His minions grew in number as did his herds of woolly fussiness. He began to call himself 'Don' Hernandero. He began to behave like a feudal ruler.

Then, one night, Hiram Swithin and his owlhooters, and his brothel-wagon and his gambling set-ups descended on Terida. There was trouble at first. But Don Hernandero was, above all, a shrewd businessman, and Swithin had a proposition, backed by *mucho dinero* (and more to come, more to be made) for him; and the Don thought about it and then fell in with it.

And thus Terida became Gamblers' Town with the sheep way out so nobody could smell 'em except the peon herders. And the settlement became dedicated to chance and to profit, a fortress for the shills and the sharp-eyed gentry, the madams, the owlhooters, the drifters, and the suckers with more money than sense.

But Marshal Amos in his cellar that smelled of apples didn't know all of this and, as his headache eased and he became permanently sure that he hadn't suffered any undue damage to any other part of his anatomy, had time to think and struggle and berate himself for being 'so goddam premature'. Like a colt with a burr in his ass. Wouldn't he ever learn?

He couldn't hear anything. His cellar was like a large tomb.

He wriggled about, moving along on his butt, until he found a wall which was opposite the high grating which wasn't large enough to let a possum through even if he could break it in. It didn't give much light either. He figured there must be a door also but he hadn't been able to find that yet. He leaned against the wall, getting his breath back after his exertions.

The floor as he had squirmed uncomfortably over it had been bare and gritty. He hadn't found any apples.

The wall seemed to be of 'dobe, maybe stretched over mud. He wondered how deep under the ground he was. The place was like a grave.

He was gratified to learn that the wall was rough and uneven. Squirming along like a big, brokenbacked tarantula, he found a place that seemed to be rougher than the rest, with jagged bits, and he began to work on the rawhide that clamped his wrists.

It was tough but it wasn't impregnable: it began to fray, loosen.

He raised himself upwards, rubbing all the while, the sweat beginning to run down his face, cling inside his clothes. Then he was upright on his feet and the bonds on his wrists parted completely with a small snapping sound and hissed to the floor.

He tried to bend and the effort made his head spin, bringing giddiness. He raised his hand. His hair was gummy, bloodied. There was a swelling, a gash. But the blood seemed to have stopped running.

Jackass! He should've stayed on his butt!

He let himself down again, and then he worked at the bonds on his ankles. As the life came back into his tough fingers, his strong arms, the task became easier and soon he was free.

He moved along, keeping by the wall, and almost fell headfirst over a short flight of stone steps, staring down at them, seeing them take on a dim shape. And there was a pile of something against the wall just past them.

He skirted them, bent.

Apples, lying on straw. He still didn't like the smell much, the *pile* of it. But he realized he was hungry. He picked up a round fruit which was new and firm and he bit into it. The juice ran into his mouth and soothed his parched throat. It ran down his chin, past his collar. He decided he kind of liked apples after all. He finished the first one and took up another, munched it as he climbed the steps to the narrow door. There was a latch and it was lifted easily but the door, a stout one, wouldn't budge, was obviously bolted on the other side. There didn't seem to be any keyhole.

Amos pressed his ear to the door and he heard something.

Something moving on the other side, the sound coming and going like the waves of a river in the wind. Scraping footsteps? Voices? A gabble? Animal noises?

Amos sat down on the top step and leaned his head against the door. He had already searched his person. His weapons were all long gone of course. He couldn't find anything sharp, nothing at all that he could use ...

Maybe he drowsed awhile—he didn't know. The sound of the bolt being shot back on the other side of the door was like a gunshot.

Amos dropped back down the steps. He picked up a couple of apples in each hand. He crouched back against the wall beside the steps.

There was a man who seemed to be alone. Amos smashed the apples in both hands against the man's face with all the force he could muster, all the rage that drove it.

The breaking fruit half-stunned the man; the pulp half-blinded him. He staggered, clawing at himself. Then he fell headlong down the steps, hitting his head on the bottom one with a thud and cartwheeled, came down in a contorted position on the cellar-floor and became still, light coming through the door bathing his dark Mexican face, the eyes squinched shut, the mouth grimacing.

Past the light somebody shouted something in Spanish: Amos didn't get the gist of it.

The unconscious man hadn't even carried his gun as he opened the door, maybe had been ready to draw it. But it was still in its holster. And Amos lifted it.

He went up the steps and eel-like through the door. On one side, his shoulder brushing the stout, rough wood, the gun at the other side of him, ready in his hand, pointing.

There was another Mexican in the small room that looked like a tackle-stores. A small man in a small room. A small man with a dark, vulpine face and shocked and staring eyes; who reached for a pearl-handled gun in an ornate holster.

Amos shot him in the face, saw the blood bounce; and then the man, gun undrawn, was on his back, almost hidden by a bridle which he had brought down from the wall as he fell. Amos went past, through another door that was half-open.

He was in a sort of lobby and, ahead of him, were more steps. He was still underground. Pausing, he wondered whether the single shot had been heard. The gun he held was stuck to his fingers with apple juice. He tucked it into his belt, wiped his hands on the side of his pants. Listening, he could hear nothing. He turned about quickly, retraced his steps, collected the gun from the man he'd killed.

Gun in each hand, he went across the lobby and up the second flight of stone steps which were more numerous than those that had led from the cellar into the place he'd thought of as the tackle-room. More like an abattoir now.

Maybe, he thought sardonically, he should have gone back to the cellar and finished off the first man who had been precipitated down the steps, hadn't it seemed made a sound since—maybe his neck was broken.

He went through the other door which lay at the top of the steps and found himself in a room larger than any he had seen before, though this was much more bare than the tackle room had been.

A long table and a cluster of chairs, all

of rough and mundane workmanship, were pushed against the wall. The rest of the floor was bare and clean. Maybe this had been a feed parlour for the help. There was yet another door, closed and silent.

Amos figured that the two Mexicans had been sent down to fetch him, thinking him still trussed like a turkey. They'd been one behind the other, not expecting any trouble.

Amos went through yet another door— this place was like a sort of warren—and came face to face with a Mexican girl whose moccasined feet had made no sound at all. She opened her mouth to scream, her fine eyes wide with shock. He quickly stashed one gun and, with his free hand, grabbed the girl around the waist, jabbed the other weapon into her soft belly. 'A noise an' I'll kill you,' he hissed.

She understood. He had never made war on women, didn't intend to, but she didn't know this. She had quickly gotten over her shock and looked at him defiantly.

But, her red, full lips pursed, she nodded her head.

She was about twenty years old and a real beauty. Her body was soft; her breasts leaned against his arm.

Amos looked about him. This room was of about the same size as the one he had just quitted. There was furniture, too, more of it and of better quality, a long table in the middle of the floor and chairs around it and plates and cutlery and cups and jugs laid out. A dining hall. And was it waiting for the diners!

'Sit down, *chiquita*,' Amos said and, almost demurely, the girl did as she was told. But still her fine eyes challenged him.

Her red lips opened, revealing white, even teeth. Her magnificent breasts rose and fell. Clad simply in a white shirt and a brown linsey skirt belted tightly at the waist, she was still a picture of young, wholesome female pulchritude. She spoke and her words surprised him.

'You are the Anglo gunfighter who killed Ben Drill and brought him in and asked for his friend Greeley. They are peegs.'

She talked pretty good Americanese. Amos asked her, 'Where is Greeley? Those two bushwhacked me. I want Greeley.'

Fifteen

She said, 'I cannot take you to Greeley. I do not know where he is. Maybe he has left this place again. But I will get you out of here if you take me with you and take me to my cousin who lives in Sante Fe. They will look after me.'

'I can do that. But what's been keeping you here?'

'Lots of girls are kept here. We are watched all the time. No man will dare to take a girl out of here, unless she is of no worth. But these people used to sell "the bad ones", as they called them, to the Comanches and the *comancheros*—and now they can be sent, too, to the brothels over the border if they are not wanted or do not behave.'

Amos said, 'Greeley or no Greeley I'm

not about to stay here as a captive. I can always come back, and I will do. You know a way out?'

It was a question and she answered it, echoed it, 'Yes, *señor,* I know a way out. I have never tried it alone. They would probably have caught me and then what happened to me would be very bad.'

'Did you hear a shot, just a short while ago?'

'No,' she said.

So this place, made it seemed of thick 'dobe, must be mighty soundproof, Amos thought.

He had both his guns in his hands now and the girl rose and led the way.

They went through a huge kitchen. Amos had seen similarly appointed places during the Civil War. Startled faces watched them, but nobody got in their way. A fat Mexican girl called out, 'Carletta': this was obviously the name of Amos's beautiful companion. She did not pause or reply. A fat swarthy man came through the end door, face running with sweat, eyes popping. Carletta snarled at him, calling him by name. He got out of their way.

'He ees my uncle,' the girl said out of the corner of her mouth. 'He ees a gutless one.'

How many relatives? Amos wondered. How many clan members? Maybe too many. But he would do his damndest. And the girl would also. With every step his admiration of her grew, her swift reaction and her intelligence, her guts. Following her, he kept to her side, his two guns still in his hands, ready.

There was more room now. Another dining hall, bigger than the one before, bigger than the huge kitchen. Rich, with red drapes at the window, thick carpeting, dark, heavy furniture of ostentatious opulence.

Tables were being laid by servants who paused, staring at the running couple. Suddenly a huge man with lank black hair stepped in their way. Six foot six maybe and built like a fighting bull. The look of an overseer about him, needing only a snakelike black whip to finish the portrait.

He screamed at Carletta in Spanish and grabbed for her. She swerved smoothly, avoiding him. Amos swung a right-hand gun, catching the giant solidly against the side of the head with the whipping steel barrel. The man went *'Ug'* and Amos had to step back to allow him to fall. Voices were raised but nobody came to the unconscious man's aid or got in the way as the tall lean Anglo with two guns caught up with the girl, as they reached another door, an open one.

'There's a narrow open space here,' Carletta said. 'We have to cut left.'

He gripped her shoulder, one gun temporarily in his belt. 'I'll go first.' He let go. Then he had both guns again.

He whipped around the corner. 'Stay behind me,' he said and she did so. There was barely room for them to move abreast with each other anyway.

This was little more than an alley. A man appeared at the end of it which was barred by sunlight. A figure was limned against the glow, a gun glinting in a hand.

Amos fired once: mustn't waste shots. The man fell backwards. He was still squirming when the other man and the girl stepped over him. But his eyes were turning up, beseechingly, and his gun was in the dust. Amos picked it up.

'Can you use this?'

'I can.' Carletta took it from his hand.

Suddenly, they were out in the open among a cluster of buildings. Barns, outhouses. A few horses grazing, and men turning their heads and gazing curiously at the running newcomers.

But then there were others, coming from all directions, hurrying. Shots were fired. The fugitives ducked low as they ran. The girl turned and fired her pistol and a man shouted in agony, went down clutching his knee. Folks took cover in the outhouses.

A window was smashed. A rifle barrel glinted. Amos saw a dim face and took a shot at it. Face and rifle disappeared.

Somebody shouted, 'I want them alive. *I want them alive!*'

Horsemen appeared, their steeds galloping. Ropes snaked from all directions.

These were the Mexican border *vaqueros,* probably the best ropers in the whole South-West.

The girl was brought down, two *riatas* clasping her, tightening. Amos took a shot at a rider but only scored his horse's neck. The beast screamed, reared. The man was pitched to the dust, his wide-brimmed sombrero rolling to Amos's feet.

But the lean Anglo found that he couldn't shoot any more. The ropes were like snakes coiling him, pulling him. His grey eyes glared in the sun with frustration and rage as he tried to lift his arms, his guns. The girl was still. Out of the corner of his eye he could see her huddled form like a trussed animal.

A rope snaked over his head. They had tried, him and the girl—how they had tried! She had been good. He hoped she was still alive. *Goddam them!* He screamed imprecations at a horse and rider that towered over him; and that wasn't like him at all. The rope tightened round his neck, choking off his wind, his words.

Something hit him very hard on the side of the head. A gun butt? A horse's hoof? A swinging rifle? Blackness swallowed him. Tighter than the ropes. *Abysmal.*

Parley told Deke and Lionel, and Stella too, that he would be the new law in Chicken Creek, that Amos had recommended him to the town council, if they could get somebody to find him that is. Somebody had found him, and here he was. He'd run into a mess of trouble. And he didn't even have a badge yet.

Stella had said that Amos hadn't told her that their old friend, Parley, was coming.

Maybe he hadn't had time, Parley had said. Maybe he hadn't thought that Parley could be found anyway, fiddlefoot that he was: Stella should know what a fiddlefoot he was, him, Parley.

Amos hadn't told deputies Lionel and Deke that Parley Masters might be coming, taking over the sheriff's job so that Amos could shuck his honorary town marshal's badge—that was what it stood for, wasn't it?—and go back to running the thriving store he'd dubbed The Armoury. Parley had said he liked the name, though he couldn't rightly see Amos standing behind a counter for any great length of time. But he hadn't, had he? He was off on the owlhoot trail again, looking for miscreants, as Amos himself might have sardonically put it.

No member of the town council had told either Lionel or Deke that Parley Masters might be along, and the two young men, both of them of about the same age as their new chief, give or take a year or so, were somewhat peeved about this, not to say a mite cranky.

Parley had asked them to take a look at the two dead bank robbers and they'd done this. Deke had said he thought he recognized the two who'd been in the bank but not the horse-holder, just a kid. Lionel had said Yeh, maybe he had seen those two somewhere, somehow. Maybe there were dodgers on them back in the office, maybe they were notorious Wanted men. He, too, wasn't sure about the third man.

The undertaker appeared. Parley went to see the mayor, led by a councilman who had appeared, and the portly banker brought up the rear. He had gotten over his shock—the recovered boodle had gone a long way to accomplish this and a teller was recounting it while the boss sweated and bumbled, getting his sense of importance back once more.

Amos came to his senses while they were toting him up the wide steps of the hacienda, an imposing edifice on the edge of town, looking out at open land but surrounded by adobe walls like those of an army post, and built like a fortress withall.

His head had taken a lot of punishment and he must have passed out again after looking around for the girl, Carletta, but not seeing her.

When he came to again it was to find himself strapped in an armchair by some kind of thick leather belt. The armchair was well-padded, though, so he wasn't too uncomfortable, only thought that his head might fall off at any moment.

He got his eyes into focus gradually, painfully.

He saw two men in front of him, a space between them and him, seated in similar chairs with wide windows behind them so that he found he had to squint his eyes again to see them. Two elderly men with portly mien, one Anglo with flowing white hair and a walrus pepper and salt moustache, the other Mexican, hawk-featured, with a thinner, blacker face adornment, black hair that was only shot with grey, and eyes like polished obsidian.

Amos said, levelly, his head clearing like magic, 'One man who calls himself Don Hernandero and tries to pass himself off as an aristocratic Spanish grandee but is just low-class *mestizo* scum. And his partner, known as Hiram Swithin—would you believe it?—and is just a shit-eating renegade *hijo de puta* like his friend.' And Amos spat on the carpeted floor between him and the two boss-men.

Behind him somebody moved. But the Mexican elder raised a hand and said 'Stay' and the slight noise ceased. Amos hadn't bothered to try and turn his head. It was just full of wool now and he didn't want to irritate it.

The two elders opposite seemed to be glaring at him but he couldn't be sure of that. Neither of them moved. Swithin hadn't even said anything. And

Hernandero said nothing more. So Amos asked, 'Where's the girl? What did you do with her?'

And then Swithin did speak, and his voice was like gravel in a can. 'I gave her to the boys. When they finished with her I planned to hang her and leave her swinging for all to see. A sort of object lesson if you see what I mean. But my amigo here wanted a different way, so I pulled her out again. He's gonna sell her to the *comancheros* who will farm her off over the border. The don likes profit whenever possible, you see.'

The prisoner sat trussed in his armchair and didn't say anything more. So Swithin went on, thinking himself now an educated man no doubt, having the illusions of grandeur like his partner, liking to hear the sound of his own voice. A scum-hound picking his words carefully, Amos thought, the way a man like him would think an educated man would; saying, 'The don is also a great one for tradition, for ritual you see ...'

'I do not hang women,' put in the elderly Mexican, as if he was aiming to explain something, sonorously, picking his words as his partner had done but for a different reason: he had had to teach himself Americanese, used Spanish, bastardized or otherwise, on his minions no doubt, was still a bit uncomfortable with anything else.

'You decayed, sanctimonious, two-faced old bastard,' spat Amos. 'The girl would be better dead than sold to some hell hole over the border, and you know that.'

Swithin said, 'My partner is a great one for revenge also. Let me tell you something else ...'

'More goddam play-acting,' spat Amos.

Swithin ignored this, went on, 'Greeley and Brill were ordered to brace you on the trail, the straight way. Not to bushwhack you, to brace you and kill you and bring in your body. Maybe you would've beaten them anyway—we know your rep—and that was a chance we had to take. We would've got you later somehow anyway, you were walking into here. You are a very foolish man. But the don wanted Greeley and Brill to do it his way. Ritual again you see. *Ritual.*'

Swithin paused, shrugged. Then he continued, 'You killed Brill. Greeley came back. You came in looking for him. We have Greeley. He will face you.'

'*Any time,*' said Amos.

Sixteen

The adobe wall was long and old, the ground beneath it of hard-beaten dirt.

A lot of the polyglot populace of Terida was gathered in ranks facing the wall.

Hiram Swithin and Don Hernandero had places of honour in wooden armchairs, like thrones, on top of a dais. A set-up that had obviously been used many times before, a sort of arena facing the wall.

In the front of the serried crowd more folks, male and female who were notables of the town, sat on benches a little behind the two chiefs. Amos was surprised to see Carletta among these people, obviously unharmed, a tough-looking *hombre* beside her, though, gripping her arm.

Her dark eyes looked luminous. Maybe they were full of beautiful sadness. She had been brought out specially to see her champion die.

At the back of the crowd, which was now growing in its numbers, the gallows towered.

There was a whipping post in the centre of the area but this wasn't to be used. Not yet anyway.

All attention was focused on the wall and the first protagonist in the little drama of death that was about to be enacted. The tall, lean moustached Anglo who was called Amos.

There had been a growing murmur, but now that had died down.

It began again when the second pro-tagonist, another Anglo, Greeley, was brought forward, a semi-circle of men with drawn guns close to him, as there had been by his opponent, still was.

Amos had his own gun-rig on, the long holster, the worn, serrated butt of the gun poking out, the wood 'walnut' shining dully in the sunshine.

Greeley was similarly armed. Both men were by the wall. Their escorts stepped back a little to give them room but kept their levelled guns at ready.

The two men faced each other, a fair distance between them. They had to wait.

There was a menacing, ritualistic flavour about the whole thing. That had been expected. The humming noise the crowd made was getting louder, but there were no shouts.

Many rituals had been witnessed here and shouting wasn't allowed until the climax—and afterwards—before the audience moved away closely watched by the *vaqueros,* the *pistoleros,* the bully-boys, the men who carried the stockwhips and the stunning clubs they had borrowed from the Indians.

Amos's eyes were hooded but very watchful. Sidelong glances but no jerk of the head, no twist. But taking in as much as he could before the fun began.

He figured he could haze Greeley—no

problem. He had to put the man down, and fast. But he had no illusions that in killing Greeley he would be saving his own skin.

He was a candidate for the scaffold, the hang-rope already dangling, waiting.

The waiting.

He was aware that, except for the narrow gap between the two armchairs, the two chieftains, *Norte Americano* and Mexican, were virtually surrounded by armed men, some of them with shotguns.

He looked straight at Greeley, and Greeley was watching him, bent, almost half-crouched. Amos stayed upright. They both waited for the signal.

This would be a gunshot fired by one of the men who watched the prisoners, the adversaries. This one a fancy but evil-looking younker with a big sombrero and a limp, who was nearer to Amos than he was to the other killer. And killers they both were, as he and his comrades were also.

Maybe he was by Amos because Amos

was considered to be the most dangerous.

Amos had been in tight spots before, had lost count of such. But this was the tightest ever.

He had been the target all along. But he didn't think about that now; only, I've got to beat this scum somehow.

His eyes were on Greeley, on the *pistolero* with the big hat, partly—and on the wall also.

It was a very old wall, and the section nearest to where he stood, the ground, the earth, the wall, looked very well used.

He knew that the Indians had been driven from the border valleys like this one, in which the gambling settlement of Terida lay, by the American and Mexican armies, whether the latter had any business here or not.

The Indians had been driven up into the hills, but they still descended into the valleys from time to time to raid and steal and murder and take captive women and children.

Gamblers' Town was like a fortress, but even this wasn't impregnable.

The adobe wall and the ground beneath told a story. The wall was pitted, holed, crumbling, with ugly blotches like stains upon it. Ugly blotches on the ground too. *Old blood.* The blood of executions.

The wall looked as if a push at one particular point—a point that was near to Amos—would knock it over. He had one of his bright ideas, the sort that he had thought more than once might be the death of him. But he didn't dwell on that sort of figuring.

He was pretty spry really. The ritual-minded Don Hernandero had allowed him to have a hot bath in order to clean himself up after his rough passage. Two *pistoleros* had been on watch of course. Then an elderly Indian doctor—it would have been discourteous to call him a medicine-man—had bandaged the prisoner's head so neatly that he was able to get his hat on.

All ritual, Amos had reflected sardonic-ally. If he was gonna be dead, he was gonna be clean and comparatively unmarked also.

The one shot was fired by the fancy-looking younker in the big sombrero.

The signal.

Amos's next movements were instinctive, fluid, almost involuntary. Greeley was mighty fast; but he wasn't fast enough. He wasn't able to fire his gun, as it was only half-out of its sheath when Amos's single shot drilled him between the eyes. The shot snapped in Amos's head, in his eyes as he saw his adversary fall as only the dead can fall.

He heard a shouting voice. But it wasn't the beginning of a cheer.

And the words he heard weren't at all the words he might have expected to hear, or anybody else in this assemblage might have expected to hear.

'The whorehouse is on fire. *The whore-house is on fire!*'

Heads were turned as if by a myriad hidden strings.

Don Hernandero was rising from his chair, turning his head, a tall man imperiously demanding explanation. Amos levelled his gun and fired off a second shot and saw the don fall.

Amos turned swiftly, threw himself, hit the wall very hard with his shoulder.

The wall collapsed and he tumbled through in a cloud of dust, his gun still in his hand, the long-barrelled Dragoon that they had allowed him to keep—till the last.

Crouching, he scrabbled around to face the ruined wall, the gap. Fancy Big Hat appeared in the gap and Amos hit him across the bridge of his nose with the long barrel of the big Dragoon and his eyes glazed and he dropped the gun he'd been lifting.

Amos left him there, limp, unconscious, effectively blocking the gap.

Amos hit the back of town, saw black smoke which seemed to be coming from the outskirts, the way he'd come in. Hell, that seemed like years ago!

Voices shouted, the sound fluctuating. A woman screamed. The buildings, as, half-crouching, Amos ran along the backs of them, made the sounds seem ghostlike.

He had grabbed Big Hat's fallen gun and now had a weapon in each hand. But he couldn't menace anybody back here: there wasn't a soul in sight, not even a prowling cat or slinking cur-dog.

It was as if the one prisoner was dead—and that was a fact anyway—and the other one was forgotten. Was the don dead? Amos had figured he'd got the old bastard plumb centre. But it had been a long shot in more ways than one and nothing could be certain.

The screaming, roped women were being dragged behind the ponies and their Apache riders who, after rounding up the frails, had set their house on fire. The bully-boys and protectors, five in all

185

who had run the brothel, had been gutted. The tribesmen hadn't bothered to scalp them: that wasn't particularly their scene anyway. Flames licked at the torn bodies on the greensward.

Two of the corpses were headless. Wild young braves had taken grinning trophies.

The tribe screamed and chi-icked as they rode out. Some of the women were dragged. Others were taken up on to the saddles in front of their captors. Who were the luckiest? It was hard to say.

Men were out in front of the fire with rifles and a few shots were fired. Somebody said that the elderly madam had been burned alive inside the house with the charred effigy of her dog at her feet.

The marksmen were scared of hitting the girls, wholesome females that many of them had known well.

The don had been carried away from the arena. There were rumours that he was dead, but nobody yet had gotten the rights of it.

Greeley was dead. His killer had disappeared after taking the shot at the don. There was turmoil: the Apaches couldn't have created a more fitting diversion if they had planned it meticulously days ahead. Gamblers' Town hadn't seen hide nor hair of a red man—except a tame one—for a longish time, and look-outs had become slack.

In the centre of the settlement right now things were slacker still and the man called Amos was able to pick up his piebald stallion, Rags, at the stables without catching even a glimpse of the hostler.

The Indians went round the hills, making for higher peaks on the border, places where it would be difficult to track them, let alone to find them.

Amos went straight through the pass and didn't see a soul until he was away on the other side.

He aimed to go back to Terida—yes, sir! But not quite yet.

Seventeen

The light was failing when he saw the bunch of riders coming towards him. He had no cover. The plains were wide open all around him. Despite the light, an eerie quality about it, the riders must have easily seen him as he had seen them.

Sheepherders? No, there were no sheep out here, not this side, either belonging to Don Hernandero or to any other woolly fancier, whether Mexican or *Norte-Americano* or anything else.

Cowboys hunting strays? Could be.

Gamblers on their way to Terida? That was more likely. Amos didn't much like that.

But he rode steadily towards them as if he hadn't a care in the world.

There were about half a dozen or so

riders, one a little ahead of the others who raised his hand in salutation just as Amos recognized him. Amos spurred his horse forward and the two riders met.

'Parley. So they found you pretty quickly, huh?'

It was a question that didn't need an answer. But, anyway, Parley Masters said, 'I'm here, ain't I? What happened to your head?'

'It's kind of a long story. You got any tucker and somep'n wet?'

They had. They produced canteens, bully-beef *tacos*, etc.

They clustered around him. Parley, new law-dog of Chicken Creek. Half-a-dozen or so other young men, a picked bunch, all of them known to Amos, among them Deputy Lionel. But no Deputy Deke—and Amos asked about him.

Then both he and Parley had a story to tell—with additions from Lionel on the sidelines, and terse, even indignant comments from the others.

Night came swiftly.

They were at the end of the pass, could see the lights of the settlement. The fire had died. There was a quietness.

Then they heard the hoofbeats of a horse. One only, they all said. Then the rider came out of the darkness, made a startled gesture. The horse wheeled.

'Carletta,' shouted Amos. 'It's me.'

The girl gentled her mount, rode it forward.

'Anybody following you?' Amos asked.

'I don't think so. They've forgotten about me I think.' She laughed, but there was little humour in it.

'The don is dead,' she went on. 'The funeral will be soon.'

'That'd be the time to hit the town,' Parley Masters said.

'Were you aiming for any place in particular?' Amos asked the girl.

'No. Not yet.'

'Have you got what you want?'

'Yes.'

'Do you know Chicken Creek?'

'I do. I have a friend there.'

He didn't ask the nature of the friend, said, 'Go there. If you can't find your friend, go to the stores called The Armoury. That is my place. My wife Stella will be there. She'll look after you.'

'Thank you.'

'Carletta—it is nothing.'

They watched her ride away, the darkness of the pass swallowing horse and rider.

Amos said, 'If it wasn't for that girl I wouldn't be here now.'

They let their horses idle.

'We'll have to do some reconnoitring,' Amos said. 'And, naturally, I can't do that. I'm liable to be shot on sight.'

Parley said, 'I'm known. I might be spotted, watched.'

Lionel said, 'I'll go in. I know the place. Leastways, I've been in there a year or so ago. I'm not known. I can play the gullible card-fancier.'

Parley and Amos exchanged glances, and the latter said, 'All right. Come back to us about noon tomorrow.' He jerked a thumb. 'We'll be bivouacked in that hole just inside the pass.'

'I know,' said Lionel.

They watched him go in the night.

'He'll be all right,' Amos said, and he meant that.

But there was a great uncertainty in him about other things. He wasn't used to that. He didn't like that, didn't like it at all.

Then again, could he be *that* sure of Deputy Lionel, the pudgy young man whom he hadn't thought much of at first, only days ago?

Deke was in a cell.

Deke was a law deputy, had been a deputy, whatever. The jailer, Lon, wasn't sure why Deke had been slapped into a cell by the new sheriff, Parley Masters. Something about him being a wanted man in other parts. Parley and Deke had obviously known each other.

Was it all part of the terrible things that had been happening in Chicken Creek of late?

First the killing of Dealey the Dealer and Sheriff Beaky Teal. And then the bank raid and more killings, though that had seen the demise of two robbers and the recovery of their loot.

Lon hadn't known Dealey very well, the poker games in the saloon being a mite too rich for Lon's blood. But old Beaky, of Lon's own generation, had been Lon's friend. This wasn't the first time that Lon had acted as jailer here in the Chicken Creek hoosegow, most times in fact when one, or both, of the two cells were occupied, hard nuts in there or not, usually just drunks sleeping it off. Until recently Sheriff Teal had kept a good town. Until ...

But Beaky was dead now and, in a quiet way, Lon mourned for him.

But if Deputy Deke ...

Come to think of it, Lon had always considered Deke to be a decent enough young feller.

Come to think of it again though, Deke was not nearly such a long-time resident of Chicken Creek as was old Lon. He had never seemed to divulge much about himself to anybody either—and, as was the way of the West, nobody had asked him impertinent questions.

If Deke had anything to do with the killing of Sheriff Teal, as far as Lon was concerned he could stay in that cell and rot.

Nah, Lon couldn't bring himself to believe ...

Hell, he was all at sixes and sevens to be sure.

Lon was dozing when he heard his name being called.

He awoke with a start. There was darkness now. There had only been twilight before. He didn't know how long he had been in a state of non-awareness.

At first he didn't even know where he was, for his mind had been troubled.

Coming to a complete awareness, he was savage with himself. And the calling voice intoned his name again.

The call! Deke!

He rose from his sprawled state in the big deskchair with the plumped cushions (how many times had he seen his friend the sheriff dozing there?) and went over to the cell-block. The door was ajar and he went through it into the narrow passage.

Deke was in the second of the two cells and Lon couldn't yet see him. But Deke must have heard Lon's footsteps and he pushed his face at the barred door as the jailer approached it.

'I'm purely gaspin', Lon,' he said. 'Can I have some water, please, *amigo?*'

He had been very tractable, Lon thought. His voice was warm, no resentment behind it.

He knows I'm just doing my job, Lon thought. And he said, 'All right, Deke. But back off from that door first off, huh?' He had been a jailer off and on for years: he went through the motions like an old horse with old tricks.

Deke backed off. Lon retraced his steps. He went into the kitchen, found a tall glass in a cupboard and filled it at the small hand pump, letting the water gush till it was ice cold and very clear.

He wondered if Deke wanted a bite as well. But he'd had coffee and *tacos* earlier, liked Mex food it seemed.

Lon ran the refreshing cold water into his mouth, splashed it, laved his face and dried it with a convenient towel.

He carried the brimming glass of water across the office and into the cell block.

Deke was sitting on the narrow bunk against the wall. He rose and came forth tentatively, saying, 'Thanks *amigo,* that's mighty appreciated. No frettin' now, I tell you. This 'ull all be straightened out when

Marshal Amos gets back.'

Lon didn't know what to say to this, so he didn't say anything. He had the keys of the cells in his belt but he didn't aim to unlock the door. He could get the glass through the bars of the cell, though a mug wouldn't have gone through there. He manipulated, spilling some of the water, but not much.

Deke reached out to help. His hand hit the rim of the glass and it was knocked from Lon's hand, some of the water slopping on to his pants. And the hand came right on and clasped Lon's throat, the fingers tightening like claws.

Lon reached for his gun but didn't know whether he'd make it. His vision was fogged. The powerful fingers were choking him. He raised both his hands and tried to tear them away. But then Deke got his other hand through the bars, his contorted face, strained with effort, swimming like a sort of mockery in front of Lon's failing vision. He gasped for breath, still fighting the two pairs of what now felt like actual steel claws. They were choking the life out of him.

One of his final thoughts was, strangely, that the cold water was seeping through the cloth of his pants at the knees.

His *last* abysmal thought was that Deke was not at all the decent feller that he (Lon) had thought him to be.

Still gripping the torn and swollen throat, ignoring the staring, accusing eyes and the swollen tongue, all sight of these things, Deke lowered the body. He was able to unhook the keys from Lon's belt and open the door from the inside.

The door opened outwards, pushing the body with it. Deke took Lon's businesslike Navy Colt and tucked it into his own belt. He left the body where it lay and went through into the office. He found his own war-gear and strapped it on, changed the spare Colt to a position in back of his belt. He found his Stetson and put it on, then he went through to the kitchen and out the back door, which he had to unbolt, and he sashayed along the dark backs of town.

Eighteen

That end of Gamblers' Town was quiet as Lionel rode past the destroyed pile from which smoke still curled. Charred timber and other materials were in a smouldering heap, but some of the foundations made from adobe still remained in strange shapes lit by the pale moonlight. They looked like pictures of *pueblos* Lionel had seen, sepia prints from the new-fangled cameras that were being used more and more to depict facets of the Wild West, for the edification or otherwise of back-East tenderfeet.

Lionel, who came from another part of the land, didn't know whether there could have been *pueblos* here, or their builders, the ancient Indians whose names he didn't know.

He remembered the original building. It

had been a big place, and well stocked, considered by some to be the best of its kind in this part of the world, and with the greatest and most numerous, collection of nubile merchandise.

Going in, Lionel went round back of this place and didn't allow it a backward glance. There were lights ahead of him, signs of life which right now he wanted to avoid. He steered his horse around the back of some outhouses, negotiated lumpy, littered ground adjacent to two leaning privies and made directly from there to the destination he'd had in mind all along.

At the back of the cabin, the place which was the kitchen, he knew, the curtains were drawn but a thin vein of light could be seen. The back door was closed. He knocked upon it; but there was no reply. He had a sense of foreboding, was reluctant to knock again; but he did so.

The relief he felt when he heard footsteps

on the other side of the door was like a douche. But there was still a dark cloud in the back of his mind. Those footsteps were so slow, so haunting. They scraped as they stopped. There was a thud against the door.

Slowly, it opened. His gaze was clear. He saw the person he had expected to see and his relief grew. But there was still an uncertainty.

He had not expected her to be so old and bent.

It had been a fair while, but still ...

'Tante Beth,' he said.

He was right in the light that streamed from the lantern behind her, but still she peered at him as if he were a stranger—or a ghost.

'Lionel,' she said. It was still the old, sweet contralto voice.

'I wondered.' He stumbled over words. 'I came in. Things have been happening ...'

She laughed. A husky sound. 'That place

on the edge of town you mean. I haven't been in there in a long time.' She stood aside to let him enter and, as he passed her, she put her arm around his shoulders and leaned on him.

Amos had a lot to think about.

Parley had told him more as they waited with the others in the bivouac just off the pass.

As Parley had said, Amos had been the target all the while. Dealey the Dealer had just happened to be in the wrong place at the wrong time. And so had Deke probably, though he had made the most of that and become Amos's friend and, after the senseless killing of Sheriff Teal, his deputy too.

It galled Amos now, realizing that at first he'd set more store by Deke than he had by Lionel, the sheriff's own deputy and his friend.

The two hired guns, Billy T and Colehan, had been inept. If they hadn't been, Amos mightn't have been here now. He had certainly been a whole lot luckier than the late Sheriff Teal.

It was Hiram Swithin, partner with Don Hernandero of Terida, the Gamblers' Town, who had put a price on Amos's head, and now Amos knew why: Parley had told him so. That old but still young sidekick of Amos, called Parley had certainly gotten around since Amos had last seen him.

Two years before, Amos had killed Swithin's son, a big-talking gunfighter who had adopted the name Dakota Sam, although his first name was actually Weston, a name he'd hated, given to him by parents he had hated, a mother long dead from a flesh-devouring sexual complaint (she had been a cathouse girl), and a father who thought he owned the world.

He had inherited his parents' bad blood, though: he began to revel in it. He hired out his gun: he was quicker than anybody his father hired, had proved this by killing two of them. Nobody was faster than him, he said.

He had braced the man they called Marshal Amos, not believing that on the borderlands some folks called him 'Marshal Death' also, and he, Dakota Sam (Wes Swithin) had died swiftly with two bullets in his chest. The man who had killed him in self-defence had never known Dakota Sam's real name.

He had been a foolish young killer who had tried to kill too often, and through foolish pride, and had paid the ultimate penalty for that.

Amos had forgotten him. You had to forget people like that: they were ghosts that shouldn't be allowed to haunt you.

But Deke, Deputy Deke he was now—that was another matter! Had Deke known about the planned assassination of Amos? Had he, in fact, helped to set it up? He had admitted to knowing Gamblers' Town and the don and Swithin. Had he known them better than anybody could have guessed?

He had taken a hell of a chance!

Then Parley Masters turned up and Parley had known Deke from way back, real name Tag Deakin, wanted for two murders in Kansas. Parley had also recognized two of the men who had taken part in the aborted Chicken Creek bank robbery. Parley hadn't known the kid who held the horses. With them, he was long gone. But two of the robbers had died. And those first two men, Parley knew, had been old saddle-pards of Tag Deakin, and that seemed a hell of a lot more than just a coincidence.

Parley had got the drop on Deke and clapped him in Chicken Creek jail with old Lon, who had been Sheriff Teal's old friend and a sort of Dutch uncle to Deputy Lionel, to watch over him.

Amos wanted to get back to Chicken Creek. But Hiram Swithin and his Gamblers' Town had to be taken care of first.

They had no firm plan yet.

They waited.

Lionel came back sooner than they had expected him to do.

Tante Beth said, 'I suffer with rheumatism. Your ma had it too. It must run in the family I guess.'

Lionel said, 'I don't remember that. I don't remember much about those days.'

'Maybe it's good that you don't.'

Seeing her full in the light Lionel realized that apart from her disability, and that was the way it had at first seemed, she was still a very handsome woman, her face finer-lined than it used to be but with none of the ageing that he might have expected when he had first seen her move and she had leaned on him. Her large brown eyes had a sparkling, vital light in them and the humour which he remembered so well.

'I'll make coffee,' she said, and her back seemed straighter as she moved to the stove. Her head was proudly erect and he knew he mustn't make any move to help her. Her raven-black hair was shot with threads of silver.

He asked, 'Do you still sing?'

'Yes. But mostly for my own amusement and for the pleasure of a few friends. I haven't been to the place on the edge of town for a long time. They had a girl who caterwauled and threw up her legs. You saw the place?'

'What's left of it. I came in on that trail.'

'That girl. I suppose the Apaches took her with the rest. A bunch of the men have gone out already. Plenty of them had girls in that house.'

'I thought the town was kind of quiet. I was surprised.'

'Swithin didn't want the men to go. And the don's dead.'

'I know.' Lionel told her about Amos.

'I saw him. Almost everybody did. It was a show.' Beth laughed out loud. 'That man turned this place on its ears. With the unconscious help of the Apaches of course.'

'So who's here now?'

'The peons and help, who do as they're told. And some of Swithin's boys.'

Not too many I hope, thought Lionel as his Tante Beth served coffee and small fruit cakes she'd baked herself, her own flavoured recipe which he remembered so well. His mother, Beth's sister, had come from a New Orleans family where a gambler had met her, fell in love with her, married her, brought her West.

Beth, who was living then with another gambler, of French extraction like her and her sister, had tagged along: the foursome had become good friends. Lionel had been born, Beth—always Tante Beth to Lionel—and her feller, now her husband (which had pleased the family back home who had thought of her as their black sheep) had had no issue.

Lionel's father and his great friend, Beth's husband, had both been killed over cards in a big game in El Paso. Lionel's mother had died about six months later, of fever brought about by grief 'twas said. Her son, Lionel, had been virtually brought up by Beth, still 'Tante' to him, and an old maiden aunt—a sort of *duenna*—who had joined them from New Orleans (to the boy she'd been Tante Anna) who had died some while before Lionel, with wise Beth's blessing, had struck out on his own.

Nineteen

The two men came through the door without knocking, swinging it wide. The woman and the young man inside the cabin had not heard their approach: they had been circumspect.

They were both youngish, lean Anglos with hard faces and watchful eyes and, what was more noticeable, drawn guns.

'Evenin', Beth,' said one of them, with a silkiness that belied the look in his eyes. His partner, less prepossessing, didn't say anything, just scowled threateningly.

'What in hell do you two want?' Beth demanded.

The silky one said, 'We saw your friend come creeping in along the back here. Coming in like that we figured maybe he was up to no good, maybe he meant

213

to rob you or do you harm.'

Beth cut in, 'He's my nephew, you jackass. He's just a-visiting.'

'We don't know him. Mr Swithin told us to keep a look-out for strangers. I guess we better take him to Mr Swithin anyway.'

'You'd have to take me to Mr Swithin as well then,' said Beth mockingly. 'I'd like to give that jumped-up dictator a piece of my mind.'

'Come to think of it,' said Silky, looking at the handsome woman's pudgy-faced companion. 'He don't look much. Still an' all, you can't always judge by appearances 'tis said. Move, bucko.' He jerked his gun.

Beth stepped forward. Then she was partly between the two bully-boys and their would-be captive. 'I told you I'm goin' too,' she said levelly.

Momentarily, Silky looked nonplussed, like a boy confronted by an indignant schoolma'am. But his stupid-looking partner had no such qualms. He gripped the woman's shoulder and swung her out of the way. But then he ran into her nephew's fist, used like a club, slamming him across the bridge of his nose and propelling him to cannon forcibly into Silky. He dropped his gun; Silky was forced to wave his in the air while he staggered backwards into the open door, hit the jamb.

By this time Lionel, no slow-coach, had his gun out and, surprisingly, Beth had plucked a wicked-looking double-barrelled derringer from a black silk purse on the corner of the table.

Silky was staggering half-in and half-out of the doorway, his partner at his feet, blood streaming from a broken nose, his eyes glazed, his gun on the floor well away from his reach.

Silky's gun began to lower. 'Drop it,' snarled Lionel, looking murderously dangerous. Silky dropped it.

Lionel strode forward, skirting the bleeding hulk on the floor. With a vicious backhand swing Lionel hit Silky across the temple with the barrel of the gun, knocking him outside where he sprawled in the dust and became still.

The man on the floor tried to grab Lionel's legs. Beth reversed her little derringer and, with the butt, hit the man forcibly on the top of the head. He went forward on his already damaged face and lay supine.

Lionel was laughing, but not too loudly. He collected the two guns, found two more which the partners used as backups. And a couple of knives. He dragged the unconscious Silky in the cabin to join his equally unconscious friend. 'Got any rope?' he asked Beth.

She produced a coil of rawhide. Lionel trussed the two men, saying, 'I guess they'll both live.' He gagged them with strips and wads of cloth torn from their garments.

'Get some things together. I'm taking you out of here an' back to Chicken Creek.'

'All right,' said Tante Beth.

Amos, Parley and the rest of the boys came out warily to meet them. The dawn was not far away. Some of the townies knew Beth, greeted her warmly. Amos and Parley were put in the picture.

Amos said, 'We'll take that place at early light.' He chuckled mirthlessly. 'Not so much danger of us shootin' at each other.'

More hoofbeats were heard, but this time from the other direction. Not a big bunch.

Two old-timers from Chicken Creek said they had met the girl Carletta on the trail. They were seeking the posse, had learned from the Mexican girl where they were at. The two newcomers had brought tragic news.

Jailer Lon had been murdered and his killer, Deke, was on the run.

After the sounds of shock and rage had died, Amos said, almost to himself, 'Where will Deke go?'

Lionel said, 'I think he'll come to Terida.'

Amos said, 'Terida first of all it will have

to be. Then I want that bastard Deke for my own.'

Nobody argued. But vengeance would start with Gamblers' Town. The two old-timers, though they volunteered to take a hand, were persuaded to go back to Chicken Creek and take Beth with them.

They both knew Beth. One of them called her 'the lovely singin' lady'.

The clatter of the hoofbeats of the three horses died in the pass. 'Come on,' said Amos and he led his band in the other direction, his old friend Parley Masters on one side of him and Lionel, now Parley's deputy, on the other.

Things had gone haywire for Deke. But he figured he wasn't done yet, not by a long sight.

He had always been a quietish, planning sort; but things didn't always go as planned, did they?

He went through in his mind the way things had gone.

He had been keeping tabs for Swithin and the don for a long time, and he wasn't the only one. Those two were like a couple of poisonous spiders in a huge web from which they reached out on every side. Besides their gambling set-ups, the don's old game of sheep-farming—in which Swithin had a cut, of course—their whoring, their numerous shill games, they were into everything else, anything that would make a profit, and murder no obstacle, often a means to an end.

Deke had known Hiram Swithin's son, Wes the young killer who had called himself Dakota Sam. He had been a loner, certainly hadn't wanted to be just another of his widowed father's minions. He had fallen foul of the gunfighter called Marshal Amos who'd been too good for him. Young Wes had died.

News travelled fast, and the chiefs of Gamblers' Town had many minions—and Hiram Swithin was almost as feudal-minded as his partner, Don Hernandero.

His pride told him that he must avenge the death of the only son he'd ever had.

So much had happened.

The bank raid had been a fillip. If Parley Masters hadn't happened along ...!

The two chiefs still owed Deke: that was the way he had it figured. He had been their go-between for a long time. He'd had a sneaking suspicion that they'd planned to control Chicken Creek in the same way they controlled other places. But for more places they needed more men and their army-crew wasn't such an efficient army as it used to be when their bailiwick was only the border lands controlled by the people they knew, terrorized, controlled.

The would-be execution of the killer of Wes Swithin, alias Dakota Sam, had failed.

The bank raid: a tragic farce.

Damn to hell and brimstone that Parley. And goddam his old friend Amos also!

But they'd be gone now, Deke figured. They'd been swallowed by the web, destroyed. And the two chiefs still owed Deke; and he rode. He didn't take the pass, though: he used a more circuitous route and he saw nobody.

They belonged to Terida but they weren't what you might call townies because Terida wasn't really a town. It was a cross between a fortress and a wide-ranging gambling hell with, incongruously, a sheep herd grazing on the far side, the side that didn't face the hills and the border.

The Terida men, on their vengeance trail, their bid to get their women back, had come out on the border side, the side that the Apaches raided, killing the look-outs and others, taking the women, setting the whorehouse on fire. But, the men of Terida opined, the Injuns had hit the wrong place this time; they had stirred up a hornets' nest and the hornets were after them surely sooner than they would expect: a bunch of hardhats armed to the teeth, men who knew how to use weapons, men who could track, men who were used to raiding and pillaging, robbing and killing.

They didn't know whether the Apaches would go over into Mexico where many of them were hiding to escape reservation life and the white man's laws, or whether they had a camp on the *Norte-American* side of the river and the hills. There were so many hills, badlands, crazy hideyholes. And the Indians would know 'em all.

They would keep some of the women and sell the others, maybe kill those they figured wouldn't be any use to them. But these were picked women who'd belonged to by far the best bordello in the border country. They would fetch a good price in horses or other barter from the *comancheros* or the Mexican flesh-pedlars or brothel-keepers.

The Terida men, seasoned owlhooters and troubleshooters though they were, didn't relish going over the border and maybe tangling with the Mexican Army (they were always chasing Indians) or the *rurales* who were as tough and dogged as the Texas and Arizona Rangers and had as wide a bailiwick.

The Terida men hoped to catch the Apaches on this side of the border.

They hoped that luck was with them.

And thus it proved to be.

For a long time they hadn't spotted much or heard anything. And the going was rough and, when night fell, in parts perilous.

Then they heard a woman scream. Just as they saw the shapes of small craggy hills ahead of them, the sort of outcrops that abounded in these wild lands. And they split into two sections and then moved in fast like two halves of a quickly closing pincer.

There were shouts—and more screams. There was ragged fire, but it wasn't heavy, was probably coming from lookouts, two or three.

A man shouted on a high note as he was propelled from his horse, the beast startled, turning, clattering down the slope. The man crawled, gun in one hand, the other clutching a shattered shoulder. Blood ran through his fingers, black in the pale light. There was no moon, only stars like bright holes poked in a darkly azure sky.

A screaming Indian broke from the rocks waving a rifle. The wounded man shot him, stopping him in mid-air: he twisted, tumbled, disappeared in a cloud of dust.

The American crawled behind a rock, rested his gun on top of it, tried to focus his pain-filled eyes. Men were dismounting as Indians came screaming out of the rocks above. Women too, some of them in the line of fire. One of them, hit in the leg, went down, her screams rising above the cries of her friends, the high-pitched whooping of the Apaches, the slam and echo of gunfire.

Some of the Apaches had rifles, others knives, hatchets, lances. One big-chested savage, taller than most Apaches, swung an enormous war club around his head, his whoops drowning the other noises. The wounded frail had passed out anyway, was silent.

Suddenly blood gushed from the giant Indian's throat but still he swung his club, crushing a man's head. But he fell upon the corpse and his club rolled down the rocks and became part of the growing debris.

The Americans, spreading out, fired methodically with their hand-guns, better at close quarters and on such uneven terrain which became more perilous as they climbed, ducking, weaving, some of the women going past them now and taking shelter.

The Apaches had been taken by surprise but they fought like the fanatical warriors they were. It became evident, though, that they were outnumbered also, were not such a big party even as the Americans had expected.

'Finish them,' a deep voice shouted. *'Finish them!'*

Men died on both sides. Two luckless women were precipitated into oblivion. The guns boomed, awakening a hideous cacophony that rolled, redoubled, fluctuated, momentarily died, then blossomed again, evilly, to drown the Apaches' shrill whoops, and their death cries.

An Americano bent to take an Indian scalp, a souvenir from a corpse. But the dead brown figure came to life and a knife slashed upwards, almost decapitating the scalp-hunter, and white man and red died together as if embracing.

Reddish-brown bodies littered the slopes. White faces stared upwards at the stars. Women ran, some of them still screaming as if they would never stop.

An old hand sat on a rock and said, 'No cat caterwauls more than a cathouse cat.' And the firing died and the dust swirled and settled. An Indian sang a moaning death song till an Anglo put a bullet in his head.

The echoes died. In the rocks there was

the smell of gunsmoke and death which, slowly, the breeze teased away.

And silent men moved—and now-silent women waited, except one who wept softly for a dead friend.

Twenty

One member of the Chicken Creek
vigilante party had a spy-glass, a collapsible
brass and glass and mahogany instrument
of which he was inordinately proud. He
said it was the only souvenir he had of his
seafaring days. When at its shortest stretch,
it was chunky and formidable-looking and
its owner told a tale of how he had killed
a bully with it—and that was why, on his
lonesome, he had come West.

He was an elderly blowhard and nobody
took much notice of his tales. But, for an
ex-sailor—if that was what he had ever
been—he was a pretty fine rifleman.

Right now his spy-glass was coming in
handy also as he kept an eye on Gamblers'
Town, saying it seemed pretty quiet.

Darkness had brought a long pause in

his spying proclivities. But then came first light and a morning haze and, with Amos, Parley and Lionel at their head, the party rode, the ex-sailor putting his instrument to his eye from time to time, with important mien, as the light got better.

Unless the folks had suddenly changed their minds, or Swithin had done it for them, this was the morning of Don Hernandero's funeral.

The watchers, including the ex-sailor, hadn't seen the Indian-hunting party returning and figured they'd be down near the border now and maybe losing their scalps. If ever there was a good time to hit Terida, Gamblers' Town, this was it.

There were no wisps of smoke coiling from the ruins on the edge of the settlement. A faint breeze moved the dust with whispering sounds. A hunting cat spat at the humans and disappeared.

'Here's where we split up,' said Marshal

Amos. He led one party, Parley the other. Lionel tagged along with the latter. He was Parley's deputy now after all.

Parley's boys took the backs, Amos's the fronts. Parley would have liked things the other way round.

Amos was the one who inevitably would be recognized. He had only recently escaped from a hangrope here. He had killed Don Hernandero. Many had hated the don. But there were the others ...

Amos might be walking straight into another hang-rope, his men into a blistering ambush.

However, Parley knew better than to argue with his old chief, who always seemed to know what he was doing anyway, reckless or not—and reckless he was. If anybody knew how Amos operated Parley was the one who certainly should.

Anyway, out back there was something that Parley's deputy, Lionel, wanted to check. And did.

The two hardcases that he'd left trussed

like turkeys for roasting in Tante Beth's kitchen were still there. They'd been gagged to stop 'em gobbling. Nobody had walked in and found 'em; and they hadn't been able to start an alarm.

One of them was blue in the face, gasping for breath behind his gag, eyes bulging, face running with perspiration. Lionel and Parley released the two of them while the rest of the Chicken Creek bunch stayed outside, but raring to go.

Water was splashed into the gasping man's face and he was given some to drink. Lionel found whiskey and made him sip it slowly.

Parley said to the gasping, demoralized fellow, 'You're lucky you ain't dead. And, from what I heard, you deserve to be.'

The man coughed, didn't say anything as the life came back into his eyes, his face. He was the one Lionel had thoughts of as Silky, but that moniker no longer fitted him.

His bloody, stupid-looking partner was

truculent and subdued as both of them were shepherded outside, their eyes starting when they saw the rest of the bunch, watchful and determined-looking.

Parley said, 'Amos is going in the front. We'll go in the back and these two bozos can lead the way.'

Amos wasn't about to lead his men down the middle of the higgledy-higgledy apology of a main street in Terida. They split. They took opposite sidewalks.

The elderly cuss with the spy-glass and the shining new Winchester repeating rifle with which he was so adept stuck by Amos almost as close as a sticky burr on a cayuse's tail.

But the horses had been left behind, tethered at the end of the street in a disused alley which contained nothing else but stinking rubbish.

Early workaday drudges, many of them in drab work-clothes, some in serapes, were moving around hardly seeming to notice the new arrivals who moved themselves nonchalantly and, seemingly, without war-like intent.

Nobody yet had pointed at the tall, lean, moustached man known as Marshal Amos. The man who had killed two men—one of them the big *jefe*—so recently in Terida.

But things were changed dramatically, explosively, when Amos and the spy-glass man, whose name was Abe, were suddenly confronted by two hard-looking young men with levelled shotguns.

At this time Abe's rifle wasn't at the slope the way he'd earlier been carrying it, soldier-like (maybe he hadn't been a sailor after all), but semi-cradled, its muzzle pointing outwards. At that moment there was nobody else nearby. There was just Amos and Abe and the two shotgun-toting Swithin boys.

And Abe pressed the trigger of the rifle.

The one hardcase who was a little ahead of his companion received the speeding bullet at close quarters in the full of his chest. It propelled him backwards until he lost his balance and left the sidewalk, his legs kicking up. His shotgun hit the sun-baked street but didn't fire. His head hit the hardness too, very forcibly. But he was already dead, wide-eyed, then *glassy-eyed.*

The second man's eyes were just as wide, but with shock. His pressure on the trigger of the double-barrelled twelve-bore was involuntary.

The slug screamed between the two men who confronted him, and the explosion was far more dramatic-sounding than the rifle-shot had been.

Amos's draw—his hand had already been resting on the butt of his gun—was as speedy as the strike of an infuriated rattlesnake. The long barrel of his Colt was lifted, the hammer thumbed. The bullet bored into a spot underneath the man's chin and drove upwards, taking off his hat and part of his skull.

As he arched backwards, his dying spasm

made his trigger-finger contract and the second barrel of the shotgun ejected its load into the air.

The echoes rolled. There were shouts and the sound of hurrying feet.

On both sides of the street the men from Chicken Creek began to move more speedily.

Above Amos and Abe, a man leaned from a window and took a bead on them with a carbine. But there was another vigilante at the back of the two: they weren't the only ones on this side of the street: they had back-up.

The man used a hand-gun, and the sniper, white face staring, tumbled to the pockmarked street, only his heels hitting the sagging, splintered-wooden sidewalk, drumming, then becoming still.

Amos pointed, waved. The imposing white building, the hacienda, was ahead of them, and the vigilantes opposite Amos and Abe and the two other men who were backing that pair, moved along close to the walls along the sidewalk.

To attack the hacienda Amos and his party had to cross the street. Amos told Abe to stay put, cover them with his sharp-shooting Winchester.

Amos went first, crouching, then rolling as bullets bit the hard ground around him, slivers of earth biting his face, steel lead biting his shoulder, the left one, in a shallow flesh wound. There was a rifleman on a roof, hiding behind the garish false front of one of the gambling dens.

He showed too much of himself. Abe took a shot at him. He dodged. He made it good. But then he over-balanced and cartwheeled downwards to the hard street, his rifle flying through the air and landing yards away from him.

He scrambled to his feet while men on the opposite side took potshots at him, all missing. He limped into cover and they let him be, had weightier and more perilous undertakings for their attention.

Twenty-One

He was a boss spider in a big web which with great suddenness was coming apart. His partner was dead, wasn't even buried yet, and he was being besieged.

He still had bully-boys, gunfighters, some of the *vaqueros*. But too many men had gone off chasing Apaches, rescuing whores. And none of them had yet returned.

Now the enemy was hammering at his door.

There were his own men out front, others out back. The sound of shooting was becoming noisier.

He didn't know that his men at the back of the hacienda had already been dispatched.

When two men came in through the back he was surprised to see them. These were two that he thought had run away, as some did sometimes. Two Anglos. A fancy one who thought he was some sort of *caballero* and *pistolero*—though not a favourite of Don Hernandero's—and his burly, brainless partner who followed him around like a hound-dog.

There were four men with Swithin and they moved forward to greet the newcomers, for they hadn't seen them lately. The fancy one looked kind of sick, even scared, and maybe that was what warned them. They went for their weapons. But they weren't quick enough.

There were other men behind the Swithin pair and they suddenly had the whole room covered. A gunfighter who stood directly in front of the boss went for a weapon. He didn't get it halfway out of its holsters. Shots blasted and he went down.

Swithin turned and went through the half-open door of his study, which was close behind him. He slammed the door and locked it.

He ran over to his huge desk and ducked under it and lifted the special piece of carpet beneath and revealed the large trapdoor with the brass ring set in it.

This led to the escape tunnel. It had been there a long time and he didn't know who had done it. Some Indians maybe, though he didn't think Indians were usually so inventive. The hacienda had been built around it and only the don and himself had known of the existence of the hidden trapdoor.

Being a man of the wide, wild West of far spaces, Swithin was scared of closed-in places. He had looked into the tunnel but had never been right to the other end.

In his younger days, Don Hernandero had made the trip and discovered that the tunnel came out in the centre of some bluffs at back of the town and was well hidden by brush. There was no used trail back there, only sheep from time to time and a few herders.

Swithin had two guns in his belt which

was full of cartridges. He let himself down into the hole and closed the trapdoor behind him. The blackness was absolute, *pressing*.

He scrabbled for lucifers, almost dropped them. He scratched one and yellow light blossomed. He had cigars in another pocket. He took one out and lit it, hoping it would give a modicum of light when a lucifer flickered out. He hoped he had enough light to last him.

He cupped the flame with his hand and tried not to puff too hard at his cigar. He began to feel his way along. The walls of the narrow passage were of slimy rocks, making his flesh crawl as, half-stooping, he moved along between them, brushing them, leaning against them as he paused to make more light.

While his men disarmed the demoralized gunfighters, Parley Masters broke the lock of the study door with his gun and crashed through almost on his knees.

No shots blasted at him. The room seemed to be empty.

He crossed to the big desk. Would a man cower there? A man like Hiram Swithin!

Parley crouched down beside the desk, the cavity, poked his gun in. Nothing happened. He was mystified, felt foolish.

He ducked his head under and saw the disturbed carpet. He found the trapdoor and lifted it and dropped down into the dark cavity.

There seemed to be some sort of a glow ahead, flickering. He ought to tell his men where he was. But there wasn't time for that. He went ahead.

Should he blast off a few shots towards the source of that fluctuating glow? He decided not to take the chance on bringing the tunnel roof down on his head, entombing him. The glow disappeared.

He didn't take a chance of lighting up himself but felt his way along. There seemed to be a bend in the tunnel, a hard place. He negotiated this, narrow, suffocating. He saw the glow again. And then, once more, it disappeared.

Hiram Swithin was a man in a panic. But then he saw the daylight ahead and he clawed at vegetation and broke through and the morning sun hit his eyes and the air was like wine.

He came out of the gully and found himself surrounded by sheep.

Sheep had been Hernandero's business not his. He hadn't known there were so many sheep out here in this particular place. They were like a shifting woolly mass and their smell assailed his nostrils. He had been a cattleman and like most cattlemen he had always hated sheep.

He ploughed through them, listening to their stupid bleating, choosing the direction which he thought was best. He had to find a horse.

Suddenly a dirty, grey-woolled ram butted him in the ass, spinning him around. That was when he caught sight of the man coming out of the brush and, at first, couldn't believe his eyes.

The truculent ram moved away from him and he drew both his guns. The shifting of the furry, stinking creatures made aiming difficult. He put one gun back in his belt and used his free hand at his wrist to steady the other one.

He saw a puff of smoke but didn't hear much. There seemed to be too much noise of the sort he wasn't used to. Something punched him in the throat. Like a butting. But the ram wasn't near now and, besides, the pain, suddenly blossoming, was too high up for a butting.

He tried to lift his gun but it seemed as heavy as an anvil and it was pulling him down.

The blood welled up into his throat and it was viscid and hot and the heat began to envelop his body, searing it. He fell among the sheep and the last thing he knew was their stench in his nostrils.

There had been a wall of steel out front of the hacienda but now it was losing its strength. These were not soldiers, or members of a posse or some sort of tribe or well-organized bandit gang. They were paid gunslingers. One of their paymasters was already dead: they were supposed to turn up at his burial service today. Now the rumour was that the other paymaster had lit out. Two of their number were dead, and more back in the street. Before their horrified eyes another was shot in the belly by the tall moustached man with the long-barrelled Dragoon who seemed to hit everything he aimed at.

Some of them ran, managed to get horses. Others sought cover in the hacienda, which was the worst thing they could have tried. They were captured by men who came in behind them.

Those who got away used the back end of town and went through the sheep meadows, ignoring staring herders. They did not spot the young man who stayed hidden in brush till they passed and then rose and walked back to town where resistance was at an end.

'We can't string 'em and take 'em all back to Chicken Creek. Let them have horses but no weapons, and drive 'em out to the border. Let 'em pass the bodies, leaving 'em lay; let 'em see what will happen to them if they delay. They're lucky we don't put 'em against that long 'dobe wall and mow 'em down.'

This was Amos's pronouncement and it was more than a just one. The living and the wounded went with alacrity and one or two whispered things like 'that's Marshal Amos and he always means what he said: he killed Greeley and the Don'. But all of them remembered him all right and always would.

They were gone. And then the victors left Terida in the other direction, carrying two bodies and two wounded and, at their head, was Amos, Parley and Lionel.

They were between the settlement and, roughly, the pass through the hills when they saw the rider approaching. He evidently hadn't actually come through the pass but around the edge of the hills and was approaching the settlement from a different direction, off the usual trail.

Old Abe, unhurt, spry as a cricket, raised his spy-glass to his eye.

There was a dramatic pause, and then Abe said, 'It's that murderous young bastard calls himself Deke.'

Amos and Parley both kneed their horses forward, glancing at each other.

Amos said, 'You got Swithin. This one's mine.'

'All right.'

Amos turned his head. 'Stay back, all o' you, understand?'

'They'll do it,' said Parley.

They did.

Amos rode to cut off the rider and his mount. The man reined in. It was too late for him to run. But did he want to?

He was recognizing his man, weighing him up. He began to ride forward again.

He went low in the saddle Indian fashion. But Amos could play at that game. They were like trick riders at a tournament, both setting their horses at a gallop at about the same time.

Amos took off his hat, hooked it over his saddle. Deke fired and the slug went past Amos's horse's neck. The piebald stallion called Rags merely snorted and kept going. But, his reins jerked, he swerved when his rider wanted him to do so.

Amos fired. Deke hadn't taken off his hat; the slug did it for him, sailing it away with a hole in the crown which, if a mite lower, could have taken a slice of Deke's skull with it.

Amos's manoeuvre had brought him slightly broadside to his opponent and, momentarily, he had somewhat of a better view. Swiftly, he made use of this.

The next shot hit Deke low in the side, not a fatal wound but one that made him sway, clutching his reins with his free hand, grasping his gun with the other as he fought to stay in the saddle.

Straightening himself convulsively, he wasn't so well hidden and another slug got him in the shoulder. But still he managed to hold on to his gun. He tried to use the old Indian rider's trick again but his body wouldn't respond now to the command that was in his mind.

The third bullet hit him in the side of the neck and Amos was nearer to him then: the spinning lead almost took Deke's head from his body.

He pitched from his saddle, fell on his face, became a ragged bloody thing lying very still.

The posse caught up.

Amos said, 'Leave 'im for the buzzards.'

They took the spare horse.

As they reached the pass they looked back. They saw the bunch approaching Terida from the direction of the border. Abe used his spy-glass again, said, 'It's the bunch with the girls.' He snorted with humourless laughter. 'They look purty-well knocked-out.'

Amos said, 'Let 'em be. There's nothin' there for them now. That's gonna be a ghost town.'

Folks talked for a long time afterwards about the battle of Gamblers' Town and the final exodus from the place which became little more than a spirit-haunted burial settlement, a sprawling graveyard, an area of ghostly sheep with ghostly herders tending them ...

This Large Print Book for the Partially sighted, who cannot read normal print, is published under the auspices of

THE ULVERSCROFT FOUNDATION

THE ULVERSCROFT FOUNDATION

. . . we hope that you have enjoyed this Large Print Book. Please think for a moment about those people who have worse eyesight problems than you . . . and are unable to even read or enjoy Large Print, without great difficulty.

You can help them by sending a donation, large or small to:

**The Ulverscroft Foundation,
1, The Green, Bradgate Road,
Anstey, Leicestershire, LE7 7FU,
England.**

or request a copy of our brochure for more details.

The Foundation will use all your help to assist those people who are handicapped by various sight problems and need special attention.

Thank you very much for your help.
